The Moon in the Water

BY THE SAME AUTHOR

Fifteen
Zillij

The Moon in the Water

AMEENA HUSSEIN

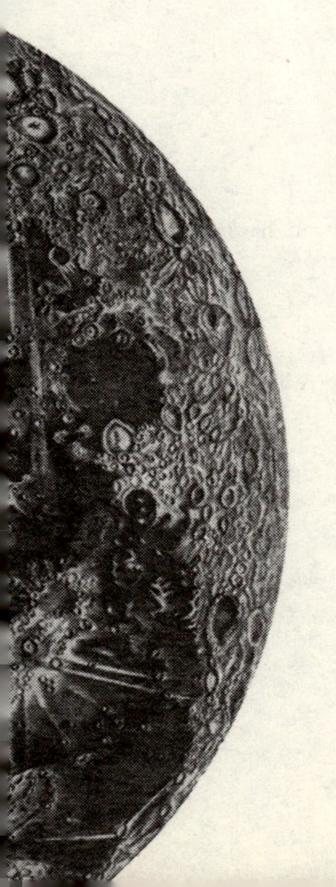

Perera Hussein Publishing House
COLOMBO

Published by the Perera-Hussein Publishing House, 2017
First published by the Perera-Hussein Publishing House, 2009

ISBN: 978-955-8897-17-1

2nd print run: 2011
3rd print run: 2017

Typeset by Deshan Tennekoon
Printed and bound by Thomson Press

To offset the environmental pollution caused by printing books, the Perera-Hussein Publishing House grows trees in Puttalam – Sri Lanka's semi-arid zone.

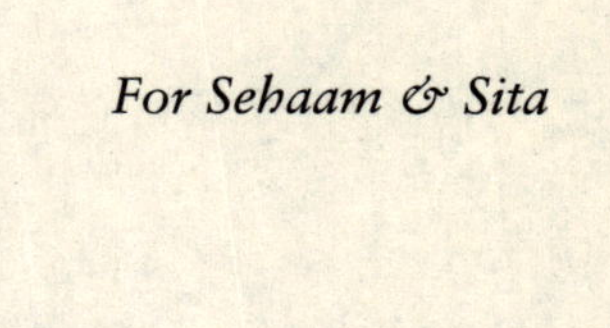

For Sehaam & Sita

Her first thought was that she was dead…and then the pain began. Her body arched into a curve of protest. Her mind snapped with the sting of electricity on her chest. Later, as she examined the burn marks below her breasts, she wondered if the scars would leave her memory.

Family?

None.

Friend?

None.

Have you taken cocaine?

Silence.

What have you taken? How much? Jesus, speak girl. We are here to help you.

Silence.

Code Blue. Code Blue. Code Blue.

Look for the Moon in the Sky, not in the Water!

JALALUDEEN RUMI

1

My father is dead.
Can I say it enough times so that it will sink in?

My father is dead.
Can I keep the pain at bay for just a little bit longer?
For numbness to come and rescue my ability to feel.
To save it.
To store it for another time.
To keep it safe for another emotion.
A happier one.

But my father is dead.

I know it and yet I push it aside so that I am able to play out the script of life. Life that demands I carry on doing the little things I did before. Go to work, meet with colleagues, ride the bus, drink some water, have a shower, go to bed.

Try to wake up.
Try to wake up.
Try to wake up.

It has not been long since he died and yet so much has changed.

My father is dead. He didn't die in his sleep. He didn't die of a heart attack. He didn't die of a long illness or a short one.

He died brutally.

Killed.

Ripped apart by a bomb.

He lay on the street for hours before he was taken away. His broken body open to the elements until a poor shopkeeper unable to bear the indignity, tore down his curtain and draped it over the dead man. My father.

Death and killed. Those two words seem to be intertwined these days. You turn on the news. There is death and killing. You read about countries. Death and killing. You hear about organizations. Death and killing. One day the world will know of death only through killing.

Khadeeja was in Seville when her father died.

'Fly to Barcelona and I will take you to Granada,' said Abdullah and before the sentence left his mouth she was winging her way to Spain. Khadeeja was not brought up with *Spain* in her vocabulary. It was always England, France, Italy, Germany and as she got older - America. *America. America.*

But Spain was the country of her dreams. It was the blending of colours, the expunging of histories, the sigh of the Moor.

They drove from the coastal city of Barcelona through Madrid and the white heat of Extramadura towards Seville. As she dozed through changing landscapes and temperatures, Abdullah sang love songs that blew out of the window to curl around the capricious dust storms that twirled frivolously beside them.

I finally found someone, that knocks me off my feet dah... dum... de dah ...dood ...aaa...de... daaaa...

I finally found the one, that makes me feel complete di...da...dum... di... da...di...doo...da di dahhh...

La...di...dah...dum... we started out as friends
It's funny dum..da da.. the best things begin...

As he sang the last line he looked at her with his black brown eyes opened wide, his mouth an oval, his hand upon his heart and she turned her head trying to suppress a smile of embarrassment at this exuberant declaration of love.

Twelve hours later, they came to Zafra. That night, in the ancient castle of the Duke of Feria - now a government run Parador - they dined like princes and as excerpts from *Carmen* swirled about them under a starlit sky, Abdullah proposed.

'Khadeeja,' he said, as he gulped down his wine, 'Love of my life, beat of my heart, rose of my garden, foam on my beer, cherry on my ice-cream sundae, will you marry me?'

She looked up at the courtyard framed sky, the minaret like tower and the arched corridors, from her seat beside the gurgling fountain and thought she could be in paradise.

She sipped her Gazpacho but didn't reply.

Two days later, while walking through the mezquita in Cordoba, between red and white columns of faded power, amidst remnant prayer, she accepted.

By that time however, her father was already dead.

It is a terrible thing to hear of a death, delayed. Every little detail of where you were and what you were doing when that death occurred is recalled and mulled over.

Khadeeja cannot remember anymore, much of Cordoba or Carmona, Cuenca, Zafra, Trujillo or any of the other magical places they travelled through.

All she remembers was that she was in Seville when her father died.

It will always be with her that while she walked through the

Mudejar Palace, the Alcazar in Seville marvelling at what she thought was a shared history with Abdullah, her father was wracked apart by a violence inflicted by another human being who also believed in his history. While she stared in awe at the magnificent cathedral, people gaped at his body lying torn and twisted on the street. As she meandered through the streets of the Barrio de Santa Cruz, buying souvenirs and choosing artisanal hand painted tiles, his blood stained the corner like a reminder that would never go away. A country's history, she reflected bitterly, is always written in blood.

⌒

Like one obsessed, she reconstructed the fateful event. Through conversations with others, by scrutinising newspaper photographs, she recreated the path of the bomb victim. Over and over again she went through every little detail until it was as if she had been there. With him. She accompanied him on his wobbly bicycle down Duplication Road, gave a cheerful wave at the dhobis who had laid out their washing on the grounds opposite the Beira Lake, sailed behind the Colombo Plaza and continued down the road that bordered the foul smelling green waters of the beautiful lake. Glanced at the shanties on the other side, at half-clad children flying kites and chasing hens, who would soon dash out to the top of the lane to gawk in horror at the remains of a man on a bicycle and the suicide bomber who killed him.

⌒

Long after, when she had returned to Geneva, while she rode the bus to work or walked on the shores of the Lac Leman, as she washed dishes or gazed up at the Mont Blanc doing the most ordinary of things, she saw that image of a man stripped by death down to the bare necessities. She saw his lifeless hand, graceful in death, having slipped out of its temporary curtain shroud, gently lie curved on the street. His bent head showing the humility he often showed in life. His very posture a symbol of non-violence. His unmarked shoes, his intact wallet, his watch un-shattered but frozen at 9:08 as if to immortalise that eternity of violence.

2

When Khadeeja was eight, a saffron robed astrologer plucked from the Colombo streets predicted she would meet a man: black – he said cryptically, at a party, who would be drawn to her like a moth to a flame. Her parents interpreting *black* to mean black hearted, warned her against liaisons with any men she met at parties. They closely chaperoned her and edged themselves in between her conversations with them. They lectured her on the theme of Men Only Want One Thing - and sent her out thus brainwashed to America to be educated, and then approved smugly of her immediate employment across the ocean in Geneva. There, in the city of peace, at a human rights conference reception, Khadeeja met Abdullah - the African from Malawi, whose beautiful black skin had the touch of velvet against steel and whose voice had the texture of soft butter.

⌒

'Esta Japonesa, la señora?' asked the nun in a quavering voice.

Khadeeja shook her head and said, 'No.'

'Then where are you from?' she continued.

'Vengo (estoy) de Siri Lanka.'

'Where is that?' she countered.

'A little island. In the Indian Ocean.' Khadeeja paused. 'India? You know India?' Her voice took on a distinctive Indian accent, her eyes widened in what she hoped would be a Bharata Natyam dancer's expression, her neck jerked and her arms stretched out to indicate its vast expanse.

'Si, Si, India. Esta Indio!'

'No una isla al sur de India.'

'Ah!' she said uncomprehendingly and continued. 'We have two Indian nuns with us. They are both small like you. *Estan pequeñitas e marron.'* She laughed kindly and the other visitors to the convent laughed with her.

'Imagine that!' Khadeeja later said to Abdullah. 'Two small brown Indian nuns have found their way to Trujillo. *Trujillo!* A one horse, no, make that half a horse town, beckoned far across the seas and land, speaking of Christian salvation and redemption and two small brown Indian nuns answered the call.'

'Deeja!' Abdullah chided softly. 'Don't be wicked. You know she was referring to South American nuns. Besides, she most probably has never seen a Japanese before and as she couldn't place you, thought you must be one of those talked about tourists. You *have* a camera hanging around your neck after all.'

'Look at these houses Abdullah!' Khadeeja said deliberately changing the conversation as they walked down the narrow street, pointing out front doors slightly ajar that revealed a riot of colour within. Tiles plastered extravagantly from floor to ceiling, swirls and whirls of plaster danced through arcs and columns.

'These,' she declared emphatically, 'are Beruwela houses.'

Abdullah looked askance and she was forced to explain.

'In Beruwela, a southern coastal town in Sri Lanka, there lives a large community of richy-rich Muslims. They struck gems some years ago and their expression of wealth was unlimited. They drove big cars, wore gaudy, brightly coloured clothes and built tasteless swirly whirly houses. We Colombo Muslims looked down on them.'

Abdullah raised his eyebrows in a voiceless question.

'S'true!' she said shrugging her shoulders unapologetically in response and continued.

'Then I come here and find myself oohing and ahing over the remnant Andalusian architecture that looks as if it is straight out of Beruwela. Look at these colours - bright green and yellow juxtaposed with blue. Look at these stairs a melee of geometric shapes...Who knew! I mean *who* knew!'

Abdullah, who had never visited Sri Lanka, let alone Beruwela, could only grunt in reply. 'Come Dheej,' he persuaded her, 'let's go and drink a *Horchata*.'

'That too is Beruwela,' she continued her torment of Abdullah as she allowed herself to be dragged by her wrist through narrow and cobbled streets, 'the same milk drink, the same base of ground nuts, the only difference is that the Beruwela Muslims would colour it bright green or pink and call it *Sharwath* while here they restrain themselves to *au natural*.'

Khadeeja looked after Abdullah who had left her behind mid-sentence, in his search for a drink. Sometimes, she thought as she eyed his tall lanky figure strolling before her, she would have liked to have had a relationship with a Sri Lankan man. It was tiresome to have to explain everything from the simplest cultural reference to what you ate, to how you ate, to how you pronounced words. Sometimes she wanted life to be simple and uncomplicated and for someone to understand her.

3

'You are living with a man?' they asked disbelievingly.

'Yes!' she replied.

'You are living with a man? A *black* man?'

'Yes,' she said again.

'Are you mad child?' they asked.

'No,' she replied more interested in how they had got to know.

It is a sad fact but true that most parents do not know their children very well. Children on the other hand learn quickly about their parents. They observe, they evaluate responses, they know what should be told and what should be kept hidden. It's not deceit, it is done to protect. Children too protect their parents.

Khadeeja shielded her parents from the knowledge that she was living with Abdullah the African from Malawi because she knew they would not understand. They had lived in different times, in different cultures, with different values. In her world there was no living in sin, no eternal damnation, no respectability in marriage. Anything was possible. In their world everything was impossible.

'Why buy the cow when you get the milk for free?' her father would constantly exhort as an example for pre-marital sex ending in the woman being used like a rag and discarded without the respectable shroud of marriage.

'*This* cow is not for sale,' she would retort, 'and does not want to be bought.' And she would see in that slight flicker of unease across his face that he could not understand. Her generation had the burden of being the link between the old world and the new. Between pre-man in the moon and post. Between letters and e-mail.

⌒

When Khadeeja met Abdullah she was engaged to be married to a man she had known all her life. Her parents knew him and his family. Their grandparents had done business together. It was the done thing. 'We are modern, broad-minded Muslims,' her parents told her at the time of the engagement as they bundled up her sleeveless dresses and shoved them at the back of her cupboard. 'You are so lucky! You *know* the boy,' they said of the young man she had seen frequently but never had a conversation with. 'You can even go out with him,' her father chuckled while her mother muttered 'Suitably chaperoned of course.'

'Such a nice boy,' people would come up to her and say. 'What a lucky girl you are!' Silently within her she waited for someone to come and tell her that she was a nice girl and that he was a lucky man to have found someone like her. No-one did. 'But Dad, I don't think he reads and Mum I am not sure, but I think he parties hard.' Khadeeja's protests were soothed. 'No Darling! Those are just wicked stories. People are jealous. They just talk. He is a really nice boy. And of course he reads! I saw all those American magazines – *Time*, *Newsweek* in their house and do you think we will give you to him if we didn't think so?' 'But do you think he will let me work after marriage?' 'Sweetheart! These are not important questions. That is a minor point. After your marriage sit down and talk it over with him and things will work out. Don't *worry* so much. We are your parents, we are the ones who worry.'

Khadeeja was reassured. The engagement took place.

Then, two weeks before she was to fly back to Sri Lanka for her wedding she met Abdullah. He was relating a story to the others at the reception and his voice, low and melty drew her into the circle and soon he was telling the story to her. For her.

'... hot September day; the heat shimmered from the ground and the air wrapped itself around like a winter coat. My rust bucket of a car was close to giving up the ghost and at Karonga I knew I had to do something about it. I saw an establishment with the grand name of Stardust Nightclub. An old, decrepit man was fixing an even more dilapidated mass in front of it.

'Good Sir!' I hailed him, 'where can I find a mechanic who can take a look at my car?'

The man gestured to the side and I saw a lopsided sign that read 'Welder' and right beneath it a third sign that said 'Bar'. It transpired that I had the good fortune to stumble upon a three-in-one establishment where I could have a drink while my car was being tinkered with and have a boogie to boot if it needed to be kept overnight. I settled myself into the reed structured drinking station and sipping a *chibuku,* I watched the old man hurl himself under my car and disappear.

Except for an evolution of grunts, wheezes and creaks, which left me in doubt as to whether it was the car or the man who needed more urgent attention, there was no one in sight.

Suddenly, seemingly from nowhere, I saw a tiny little girl take the turn around the *chibuku* shack. She wore a thick zebra striped woolen coat and held both arms straight out at shoulder level. She was holding something in her hands. As she came closer I saw that she gingerly held by thumb and forefinger a nestling weaver bird in each hand. These birds are a delicacy in those regions and no doubt she must have congratulated herself on her good fortune at snaring not just one but two of them. Then, just as she had passed me and was moving out towards the road into town, a pair of bright canary yellow panties fell from beneath the coat to her ankles. She stopped. She didn't look back at me even though she had seen me planted by the shack. I could feel her dilemma.

After a few minutes she resumed her journey, inching along, her panty shackles allowing a shuffle. The memory of that little girl shuffling down the dusty road towards Karonga town, holding a pair of weaver birds, girdled by her canary yellow panties, will always remain with me.'

Abdullah paused and as the imagery of the story seeped into his listeners he took a slow sip of wine.

'You didn't take a photograph?' Khadeeja's question sailed clear over the heads of those closest to Abdullah.

'No,' he replied and looked for the face of the voice amidst the sea of expressions and then finding her stared straight and hard.

'Why not?' she baited. 'You could have sold it to *Time* or *Life* or *National Geographic* and exoticised the moment for ever, not just for you but for a million other people.'

The others around them sniggered and waited for Abdullah's reply.

'Don't worry,' he said in his thick black velvety Malawian accent. 'Don't worry, if it had been a little white kid I would have taken the photograph. But this! This is nothing out of the ordinary for us Africans.'

There were more sniggers as he walked towards her and took her by the elbow. 'Come with me ...'

She looked startled.

'... for dinner.' he finished his sentence with a smile. 'I'm tired of these intellectual all talk boring encounters. I like your spirit young lady. Come on, we can continue this feisty discussion.'

'I can't. Not tonight, I have made other plans,' she said, inwardly cursing the Sri Lankan ambassador for holding his once a year *We are Sri Lankans, let us bond* party the same evening.

'Oh! A pity my dear. I have more stories to tell. Real exotic stories of how the English drink tea and the Americans eat hamburgers. Not these half baked no colour stories of running with the bulls in Pamplona or trekking to base camp in the Himalayas.'

She laughed as she eyed him sideways flirting like mad. 'How about coffee tomorrow?'

'I wouldn't miss it for the world,' he said as he helped her on with her coat.

The next day, over coffee in the Bar de l'escargot, she discussed with him in detail her marriage plans. The day after, she showed him the dress she was to be married in that had been bought at *Thierry's*. The fourth day she danced with him seductively at the Pirogue night club to the music of Sting's *Desert Rose*. The fifth day she kissed him. The sixth day, she called the wedding off. The seventh day she moved in with Abdullah the African from Malawi.

4

Bohtal Pattarai! Bohtaal Pattarai! Ganesh wailed his trademark song as he walked the streets of Colpetty. The bottle-paper man had plied his trade in this area for the past thirty years, and knew that when he died there would be no inheritors of his occupation. The new generation did not take kindly to this type of work. It was considered lowly and inferior and now, with the city beginning a recycling program of sorts (every other Saturday, bottles/newspapers/glass) it's '*taking the bread right out of my mouth*,' he muttered to himself as he hitched the load of papers onto his cart and trundled it through the alley behind the petrol shed.

That morning as he pushed his half filled cart through the streets, he stopped cold outside the Rasheed residence. There was a *shandaak* resting outside the gate. The silver frame, shaped like a coffin was covered with a green satin cloth embroidered with Arabic calligraphy. He knew it could only mean one thing. Someone was dead.

'*Enda thangam dorai! Aiyo! Aiyo*!' he wailed as Kusuma tried to shush him pushing him towards the back door. The Rasheed residence was in turmoil since last evening when it became known that Muhammed Rasheed, patriarch and retired civil engineer was the cyclist who had been killed in the Elephant House roundabout bomb blast.

The house was filled to the brim with people. Relatives, friends, colleagues, children's friends, wife's friends, neighbours, clients and now the bottle-paper man. The story of the circumstances of his death were told and re-told, exaggerated and embellished till it reached the proportions of a Saga that went thus:

Rasheed had been cycling that Sunday morning as he liked to do on weekends when the streets were empty of cars and reminded him of the days when he was a child. *I know just what he meant men! Can't even do these simple things during this yakka kaala! Kali Yuga has come, I tell you.*

'When I was a child,' he was known to say on a Sunday, 'the roads were like this. If we wanted to go to *Cargills* we got into our car and drove to the entrance of the shop and the driver would be able to park right there. There were no parking tickets, no security checkpoints, no rude policemen, no barriers, no one way system! *So true, I remember those days, so well! (Sigh) Tchah! That was the life!*

His sarong tucked between his legs, his banyan stretched across his rice belly, he would lie back on the *haansi putuwa* with a satisfied smile on his face remembering his childhood.

But his reverie with antiquity would be interrupted rudely by his children, 'Naturally all of you were fat! What a waste of living! How dreadful to be so decadent! Sheer exploitation of the underprivileged...' And he would then softly grumble about the deprivation of the younger generation who didn't know how to live. *Very true aney, this modern generation, they don't know life the way we did! All this e-mail, sheemail! Nonsense! GameBoy, DVD and goodness knows what else?*

So he was cycling towards the Fort when at the Elephant House roundabout he ran into a man who suddenly stepped onto the road. *Aandavanay! People just cross the road, as and when they like. No discipline in this country!* That man had a bomb strapped to his body and had been targeting a convoy of army vehicles scheduled to pass by on the way to the army hospital close by. (Sharp intake of breath) *Aiyo! Paavum! Then, tell what happened will you?*

He saw the vehicles approaching in the far distance and in his excitement... *it must be no? Can be no other reason...* he stepped onto the road to detonate the bomb. These *Bloody Terrorists! I don't know what this country is coming to. It is ruined. Ruined I tell you.* He didn't see Rasheed who most probably would have been humming a Frank Sinatra tune, cycling in his wobbly way. *Haaney, If I close my eyes I can just imagine it men, in his over-sized shorts and his white tennis T shirt, white socks and shoes.* Rasheed probably didn't see him either. *So who expects a terror-ist to just pop out like that ha? Though these days you never can tell.* So there it was. One cyclist and one suicide bomber dead. People who didn't know him were thankful that the convoy of army trucks was saved.

'It could've been worse,' they said.

Those at the funeral said, 'Fine man! Lovely man! Gem of a man! Saint! One of a kind! Prince!'

5

RaushenGul had to begin her idda straightaway. As soon as Rasheed's mortal remains or what was left of them were hoisted by ten men chanting *La illaha illallah*! into the back of a lorry, which began to move slowly with a large gathering of men following in cars, to the Kuppiyawatte burial ground, RaushenGul was whisked into widowhood.

While her best friend Nelum stood beside her, much to the consternation of RaushenGul's relatives who didn't know what to do with this *kaffir* in their midst, they pushed, pulled, shoved and pleated RaushenGul into a white sari, *sans* jewellery and covered her head. All the while Nelum projected a running commentary of protest at their insensitivity and haste to rush her into secluded widowhood. The relatives began to dislike her even more.

⌒

The RaushenGul-Nelum friendship began in school on a wet rainy monsoon day the second term of Grade One, when RaushenGul shared her box of snacks with the new girl who looked lonely and friendless.

'Can I touch?' asked RaushenGul gazing with wonder upon the dead butterfly Nelum had preserved in a matchbox – a first day at school present from her gardener. She nodded and they took turns stroking the soft wings that soon turned to dust, unable to withstand the surfeit of love they showered on it. Each day Nelum would bring a different dead butterfly to be stroked and destroyed while RaushenGul in return, fed her delicacies cooked by her mother.

Muscat, *Dodol*, *Sheenakka*, *Bowl* and *Dhoshi* were exchanged for Common Bushbrowns, Lemon Pansies, and Lime Butterflies.

'Allah!' screeched her mother when she heard that her daughter had been feeding a little Sinhalese heathen child in exchange for the pitiful privilege of stroking a few dead butterflies. 'What madness has come over her? It is the fault of this Catholic school her father insists I send her to. Education! Education! They keep on saying, but for what? What is wrong with staying at home and learning to cook and sew and paint?' She hoisted her sari pota that kept slipping off her head as she counted the dates that had just arrived from Baghdad while the household trembled at her displeasure.

Sara Umma was a daunting woman who could only be silenced by her husband and that too with difficulty. She had a chin like the rock of Gibraltar which when jutted out at a particular angle boded ill and threw the household in turmoil.

Little RaushenGul was spoilt and petted by her father Muhammed Careem. 'Please Wappa, please, please, *please*,' she pleaded closing her eyes tight and holding her hands tightly together in front of him. 'I will be good and finish reciting the whole Quran this year if Nelum can be my friend.' Muhammed Careem patted his too pretty daughter on the head and thought the world is changing indeed. In my time not only did we not go to school, we were friends only with other Muslims. But today, my daughter goes to a Catholic school and her best friend is a little Sinhalese Buddhist girl. 'Of course *Mawal*,' the patriarch replied as he puffed away on his Montecristo cigar. 'Don't worry, *puff puff*, I shall talk to Umma, *puff puff*, and all will be well.' *Puff, puff, puff.*

And so, Sara Umma was forced to send snacks for two little children. Every evening with a face as long as Galle Face, she supervised the cook in the kitchen grumbling and complaining that RaushenGul needed to know that the world did not revolve round her. 'Mark my words, that little girl will be trouble when she grows up. Getting her own way, all the time. *Enna Idai Paithiyam*. What madness is this? Utter nonsense!'

Eventually the massacre of butterflies came to an end as Nelum's parents realized the butterfly population in their garden was almost decimated when the gardener fell at their feet and begged to be freed from his role of butterfly executioner. 'Everyday, Nelum baba telling kill, kill different, different butterfly. One day blue, one day yellow, today brown, next day black.' But long after the butterflies ceased and the snacks stopped, the friendship continued.

⌒

That evening while RaushenGul listened to the familiar *kaththam* prayers that were recited in the living room while Nelum sat beside her on the bed, she grieved. It was the grief of a woman who had been married to the love of her life. There were no tears, there were no cries – only an emptiness like a drought ridden well. It held the tragedy of a ruined land and her eyes reflected a loss that was complete.

6

The young and beautiful RaushenGul had many admirers and many offers of marriage. She chose instead to marry her first cousin, a man fifteen years older. Unusually, it wasn't an arranged marriage. Rasheed had been engaged to marry a young wealthy girl from Kandy. He had just returned to Colombo after graduating as an engineer in England and was considered an eligible catch. He sported an Elvis puff, had an armful of records – Simon and Garfunkle, James Brown, Led Zeppelin and The Supremes – wore flares, side burns and b-i-i-g collars and was considered the man about town and city slicker of the day.

But his seven years overseas had tarnished him with new fangled ideas of marrying for love and living away from his parents in a separate house. When he heard that he was betrothed to a girl he had never seen, he threw a tantrum and refused to go ahead with the marriage. So stubborn was he in his refusal and so determined were his parents that he marry this girl whom they knew would inject new life into their dwindling fortune that each party carried on as if nothing had changed. Muhammad Rasheed ran around with his friends, drinking, carousing and making sure their carryings on became public knowledge while his parents went ahead with wedding plans, chose furniture, made jewellery for their new daughter-in-law-to-be and printed invitation cards. However, as the wedding approached and Muhammad Rasheed was determinedly refusing to go ahead with it, a cautious elder relative summoned his parents for counsel. It was agreed with great reluctance and secrecy that a stand-by bridegroom would have to be elected. The bride's family was informed of this - ahem - small problem but they didn't think it mattered whom their daughter married as long as it was a grandson of this esteemed and well regarded family that would lend some respectability to their nouveau richness.

'Muhammad Rasheed, Muhammad Izzadeen, what does it matter?' they asked. 'It's a Muhammad after all, that's the main thing.'

The wedding day dawned, and Muhammad Rasheed was nowhere to be found. He had stolen away the previous night to his friend's tea estate in the hills. Sitting in a spacious verandah and sipping a cup of high grown tea, Rasheed was quite unaware of the stand-by bridegroom and felt twinges of guilt at leaving an innocent girl high and dry. He imagined her seated on a frothy confection of a throne, waiting patiently for the groom who was to walk down that red carpet towards her. He envisioned her desolate and crushed at her public shaming and enforced virginal state, never to be married off again, for who would marry a girl abandoned like this on her wedding day?

There must be, he imagined others saying, *something wrong with the girl*. But he spoke sternly to himself, *it is my life and I will not have it dictated to by others. I will not marry except for love. That is my rule of life.*

That night the wedding guests arrived, and witnessed a marriage. They delighted in how radiant the bride looked and how eagerly her husband gazed at her.

'What a good looking pair,' they said. 'A perfect match.' Thirty two years later, it has proven a successful marriage by any standard.

After the wedding had taken place Muhammad Rasheed came back to the family home as silently as he had left. On learning of his brother's recent nuptials he had considered ignoring Muhammad Izzadeen but his ex-fiancée, current sister-in-law was so sweet and charming to him that he decided to forgive his treacherous brother.

'I could have been forced to fall in love with her,' he was heard to mutter to some distant cousins. 'They didn't try hard enough. They could have made us accidentally-purposely meet and then I could have fallen in love and my principles wouldn't have been broken and we would all have been happy.'

But his disgusted family had had enough and decided to ignore him. They washed their hands completely of him. His parents reasoned that from now on he could do what he wanted, when he wanted and with whom he wanted. They had nothing more to do with him. He was allowed to eat and sleep at home but all the residents of the house were forbidden from speaking to him. Even the servants were allowed to ignore him.

'So! So! How! How!'

The family seated around the dining table looked at him in stony silence.

'So! What's up! Tell the latest news men! Izza, how are things? Everything ok?'

Muhammad Izzadeen looked pleadingly at his brother to stop tormenting him in front of his parents. His new bride Razana looked down at the fading henna on her palms and twisted her sari pota into the shape of a flower.

'Jane Ayah!' shouted his mother. 'Tell the driver to bring the car to the porch!'

'Ah! Going out? Good! Good! Shall I come?' There was a forced jollity in Muhammad Rasheed's voice. It had been three weeks now and he thought that he should be forgiven. Surely, they didn't intend to carry on this act for much longer?

'Come! Izzadeen! Razana!' his mother commanded in an imperious tone that indicated quite clearly that Muhammed Rasheed should be ignored. 'We shall be back in two hours, dear,' she told his father kindly and swept out of the room with the couple scurrying behind.

'Wappa!' Rasheed began to plead, when the old man raised his hand, looked his eldest son in the eye and shook his head. Rasheed stopped. He was alarmed. He hadn't realized there would be consequences.

Khadeeja's father, the apple of his family's eye, the chosen heir, the *we pin our aspirations on him*, the saviour who shall marry a rich heiress, our son the engineer England passed out, thought he was being treated rather shabbily. He couldn't deal with his new status of son ignored, and in his spare time began hanging around his uncle's house that was literally around the corner from his own. Every morning he would wake up and gulp a cup of cold tea that had been left quite indifferently on the first floor landing by Jane Ayah. After a quick shower and a deliberate clatter down the wooden stairs he would saunter nonchalantly out of the house without a word to the rest of the family who in any case were ignoring him, and leave for work. He was apprenticed at a surveyor's office down the next lane but every evening he could be found at his Uncle Muhammed Careem's house.

There he became reacquainted with his first cousin RaushenGul who had made a name in the family for being card crazy. At fifteen RaushenGul knew every card game there was to know. She was also a terrible cheat and would often make winnable bargains to her every advantage. 'Let's play a game of poker and let's see... what shall the prize be?' She drummed her fingers on the dining table as if in deep thought, her light brown eyes sparkling with mischief. 'I know!' she would declare brightly. 'If I win you can't tell Wappa that I broke the stained glass window in the drawing room.' And thus her opponent would be drawn into the conspiracy. Or she would exert her influence on indulgent junior aunts thus: 'If I win three games of rummy in a row you *have* to get Umma's permission and take me to see *Love Story* three times in a week.' Her reputation at cards ensured that there were not many who wanted to oppose her, unless of course they wanted to indulge her every whim and RaushenGul who was much loved was therefore much indulged.

No sooner had Muhammad Rasheed begun his uninvited sojourn at her house, RaushenGul cast her almond shaped topaz eyes upon him and decided for some inexplicable reason that he would be her card partner for life. The courtship began with what looked like an innocent game of pairs. Six months later the fifteen year old RaushenGul had enslaved her thirty year old cousin for life. One day he quiveringly made a proposition to her in the form of a joke. A crucial game of two person *three-nought-four* and if she lost she would have to marry him. If she won, well then he would leave their house and she never need see him again. She agreed. RaushenGul looked at her first hand with narrowed eyes and realised that she could play a game of first hand caps and win. And she did. Muhammad Rasheed pushed his chair backwards wiped his clammy hands on his trousers and rose silently. He cast a quick look at the beautiful young girl seated before him. *Oh God! What a silly bet and oh how he loved her*. As he left the house broken-hearted he heard a soft shuffle in the sand behind him, RaushenGul pounced inelegantly on him, her legs wound around his stomach, her hands held tightly onto his neck. 'Gotcha!' she whispered, and then, 'My husband.'

7

My father is wearing a green and white checked Palayakat sarong and a white shirt. He is barefoot and seated cross legged under the huge Del tree in our back garden. The sky is a beautiful blue, and white puffs of cloud float speedily up and down. My father's four children are playing around him. He calls us. He has presents. He gives my sister a beautiful gold book, my younger brother gets an ivory pen and my youngest brother gets a jewelled watch. There is no present for me. I wait on the side while the others play with their gifts. He calls me and makes me sit on his lap. He hugs me and makes me cup my hands and into them he pours some earth. Then he says, 'I have given you the world. Worth far more than a book, pen or watch. You are the one I love best of all. You are the one to whom I have given most.'

For an instant, for a fragment of time, Khadeeja forgets that her father is dead. She wakes up with a jerk on the plane. She has an hour before landing at the Bandaranaike International Airport. She cannot help it, the tears stream down her cheeks while her neighbour shifts uneasily.

She is met by her brother Saif who greets her with a tight sorrowful hug and drives her silently into the capital. They speak little. The morning congestion has started and she notices that more people are commuting to the city than in previous years. The traffic is thick. She feels strange returning to the country of her birth after many years. The slow paced island has developed a pulse of energy that spills onto the street. Sleek modern cars share space with dogs and cattle; people skip nimbly across crowded streets, courting death with huge container trucks that thunder like Mad Max down winding roads, and crows battle with butchers and fishermen who festoon their bloody trade on hooks that hang from the low ceilings of little shack shops. Shopkeepers sprinkle water outside their little boutiques to keep the dust down and incense and turmeric water scents and cleans the enclosed spaces. Housewives in shapeless housecoats water their plants and see their children dressed in spotless white uniforms, off to school. Buses lean over with the weight of passengers and gently snort exhaust fumes while stopped at traffic lights. *I'm home* she thinks. *I am really home* and the sadness she feels is tinged with joy. An exile has returned.

⌒

She walks into the house and finds her mother on the telephone. *Typical*, she thinks, as she goes up to RaushenGul, gives her a quick hug, which is tearfully returned, and goes upstairs to leave her bags in her childhood room.

RaushenGul is a telephone person. Has always been so. She has long chats with five or six people everyday, one of whom is *her* mother. Khadeeja's grandmother Sara many years widowed, and eldest aunt Yasmin, live together in their ancestral Colombo home. Sara and RaushenGul would talk or more accurately Sara would have a monologue with RaushenGul saying *Yes. Yes. Yes...* during the entire conversation.

Later, when asked what the conversation had been about,

RaushenGul would reply *nothing*. It maddened Rasheed, who had no weapon to combat a *nothing* and yet was keen to know the latest crusade his mother-in-law had taken up. One year it had been the invasion of stray dogs, another year it had been the smell caused by the pollution of the Beira Lake. That same year she took up the recent flooding of never-before-flooded roads due to the rapid build-up of the city. He knew that a few months ago it had been the lack of residential zoning in Colombo. He wondered when it would change and what the new theme would be.

'I'm sure she can be calculated,' Rasheed would tease RaushenGul. 'If I plot how often a 'cause' comes up and how long it lasts, how far it resides from her and what social profitability it has, I can come up in advance with all the possible 'causes' your mother would be involved in during her lifetime.'

RaushenGul would merely purse her lips disapprovingly while her fingers spun the dial of the telephone with practiced agility. She had no sense of humour when it came to her mother and disliked her husband's frivolous approach towards his mother-in-law.

'So, how?' she said into the telephone receiver turning her back slightly on Rasheed who hovered beside her. Knowing when he was not wanted, he wandered towards the kitchen to ask Kusuma to make him a cup of plain tea, leaving his wife to speak to her best friend Nelum in peace.

'What are you doing?' Nelum would ask. 'Nothing,' RaushenGul answered knowing that if her husband was passing by he would scowl. Here was a different *nothing* he would have to reckon with.

Sometimes when he was annoyed he would say to no-one in particular that the Oxford Dictionary researchers should get in touch with his wife for she had a whole new definition of the word *nothing*.

RaushenGul would ignore him and carry on talking with her friend. Lives were unravelled, reputations shredded, love affairs exposed and marriages destroyed. They were unashamed gossips!

⌒

Showered and changed, Khadeeja came down to find her mother sitting on a bed in the room downstairs. The tension was palpable. RaushenGul had been speaking to her mother and it had not gone well. Their latest dispute was about the idda.

RaushenGul had practical views about the custom of mourning for Muslim wives. She had agreed that she should wear a white sari for the four months and ten days of seclusion (*but where exactly does it say it has to be white?*) Refused to listen to people who wanted her to take it to an extreme and wear white slippers, white nightdresses (*in any case she said, I wear pyjamas*) and to remove mirrors, pictures and listen to prayers 24/7.

'Mourning comes from the heart,' she would say to her daily visitors. 'No-one but I know the marriage that Rasheed and I had, so no-one can come and tell me that I am not mourning him properly.'

Sometimes she would be derisive and tell her visitors, 'Isn't it a bit ridiculous to prescribe a time of mourning? And what if the marriage was a bad one, why on earth should a woman mourn? She will instead be quite happy at the death of her husband. Why should a woman be a hypocrite? What Allah hates most are hypocrites! Am I not right?' she would demand from them and they, confused and frightened would cower and seem to agree in silence. The braver ones would tentatively put forward alternative scenarios: 'But RaushenGul Daatha, isn't idda to ensure there is no pregnancy… I don't know properly but…' here the voice begins to falter under RaushenGul's unblinking and stern gaze. There is help from another quarter, a second attempt to explain. 'We have been told that idda is to ensure that if there is a pregnancy the widow will not rush into another marriage and, you know, confuse the paternity of the unborn child.' There it was said and quite well too. They begin to congratulate themselves until RaushenGul launches into an attack that decimates their reasoning and leaves them more confused than before.

'If a woman,' she begins slowly and deliberately, looking at them with sharp eyes as she spoke. 'If a woman who has just been widowed desires to contract another marriage immediately on her husband's death (here there is a gasp of horror from her listeners, which RaushenGul ignores) and if her new husband to be is willing to accept the financial responsibility of looking after the child,… then who cares about paternity? What goodly use is it? Secondly what about women like me, who are past the age of child-bearing? Of what advantage is this seclusion to us? Mourning *cannot*, must not be enforced. It makes a mockery of the very concept of sadness.'

Oh! how they hate visiting her. It is not as nice as visiting other widows, who quietly sit in their rooms, contemplating, praying, truly mourning their beloved husbands. RaushenGul's idda was not without its problems.

Immediately after the funeral, her mother Sara came to stay with her. It was not a success. Sara, in her early seventies was a strong and formidable woman. She was the matriarch of the family who wielded much power over her relatives. No marriage, funeral or naming ceremony could take place without her blessing. Sara presided over RaushenGul's idda like a tyrant ruling a country. RaushenGul's liberal and moderate attitude towards the prescribed period of mourning became a time of strict rules and regulations and after two days RaushenGul made her displeasure known.

'RaushenGul,' her mother said sternly, 'it is my fault that you have become a stubborn and spoilt woman. I will have to accept the blame of all when they say that I brought you up badly and you have become a bad Muslim.'

'What nonsense, you talk Umma,' RaushenGul responded smartly. 'Everything about Islam is interpretation. So you keep to your interpretation and I will keep to mine. Just as much as I do not force my opinion down your throat, please do not interfere with mine.'

Sara was infuriated that her daughter should dare to defy her. 'It is *not* interpretation, it is Islam. We have our ways of doing things, ways that have been in existence for generations. Who do you think you are to change them to suit your convenience?' She fiddled with her cut lawn long sleeved blouse and adjusted her sari pota on her head with a firm hand.

'Umma,' RaushenGul persisted as she crossed her legs on her bed and leant against the bed-head insolently, 'don't bring all these Hadiths and park them on my doorstep. Even Rasheed said that the Hadiths was written down 100 years after the Holy Prophet's death, if you read them you will realize that that great and wonderful man wouldn't have said most of them. Instead of relying on your own pursuit of knowledge (again a favourite phrase of Rasheed's) you rely on these half baked alims who only know to shout ignorant sermons in arabu-tamul, grow their beards long, beat their wives, force them to wear black and have too many children that they expect us to subsidize.'

Outraged, Sara packed her bags, announced publicly that her son-in-law, angel on earth while he lived had thoroughly spoiled her daughter and that she was having nothing more to do with this new fangled way of observing idda.

'That husband of hers was a saint. Is it too much to ask of her to stay inside her room, cover her head, wear white, not speak to *kaffirs*, (a pointed dig at Nelum) and pray for his soul. Now see what he has done! He has given her too much freedom and she is running like an *authutta maadu* with it.' Sari pota adjusted unnecessarily once again, Sara stood up and radiated an air of firmness.

'Now, now, Sara Daatha,' a well meaning relative intervened, 'this is not the time to call her a crazed bull, give RaushenGul some time, she will come around. The death has been a big shock for her, like it has been for all of us. Why just the other day Kamil was saying that he had met Rasheed Machchan walking briskly up and down Galle Face Green and they had watched a man catch six baby shark by just throwing a piece of string into the ocean and they just came to the man, swimming, swimming, as if they wanted him to catch them and eat them, anyway...'

'Hanim, I have no time for your ramblings and nonsensical stories. Now, I am leaving this house. I can't stay in this mad place anymore. I will come on Kaththam days and organise the whole thing, for if I leave it to RaushenGul it will be a shambles. That child does not have the faintest idea of how to do any of these things.

'I know that I will be blamed for the whole thing. People will talk. People will say that this RaushenGul is a disgrace. It will be my name that will be dragged in the mud but does she care? No! The selfish woman is only thinking about her creature comforts. I mean her husband is dead, shouldn't she observe the rules? It is common decency...'

From the safety of her room, RaushenGul watched her mother leave the house ranting and scolding. After Sara heaved herself into her ancient Mercedes Benz that would drive round the corner and deposit her in the house that was now run by her eldest daughter Yasmin, RaushenGul gave a sigh of relief at having got her own house back and began to attend to the running of it.

In the mornings Kusuma would come to get the menu for lunch and arrange for the provisions to be delivered by Yasmin's driver. In the evenings the immediate family gathered at her house to *thamam* a Quran. This was to go on for the first forty days after the death. Early evening the drawing room furniture would be pushed to the edge of the room. The red cement floor would be covered with *paduru* and around six o'clock they would sit cross-legged on the ground (old aunties with bad knees on chairs) and recite the *Ratib ul Haddad*, then *Surah Yasin*, and end with a few *baiths* and *mowloods*. Mid-way through, small coffee cups of *gahuwa* were served with a samosa on a plate. After a few chants of mowlood sung to the tune of *Isle of Capri* or *Dil Se*, the Kaththam was wound up. On important Kaththam days a family member would take charge of the evening meal. They were allowed to invite their guests and choose the menus which were special dinners of nei roti and turkey badam with chocolate pudding for dessert or stringhopper kaliyavendu, porichcha koli and wattalapam. On these days the crowd was bigger, people dressed up and the whole house took on the atmosphere of a party.

Khadeeja had returned in time for the seventh Kaththam which was being given that night by her aunt Yasmin. When the guests had gone home after prayers and dinner, a family conference was summoned. Khadeeja, her brothers Saif and Tariq and her younger sister Sabrina together with Yasmin and her husband Yusuf met in RaushenGul's bedroom. Sara, unaware of the meeting had already gone home.

'Come, let us go outside and talk. This room is too small to hold me, it certainly cannot hold all of us in here.'

Yusuf looked askance at his wife wondering if it was in accordance with the idda rules. 'What about the male servants?' he tentatively offered rubbing his balding head for reassuarance.

'Don't be silly Yusuf,' his wife rebuked, gently taking him by the arm and propelling him out of the room as she spoke, 'so what if there are male servants? You are beginning to sound like Umma!'

Embarassed at his conservatism he obediently followed the others out to the veranda that overlooked the sloping back garden. He knew that traditionally he too should not be allowed to see RaushenGul who during her idda could only be exposed to males who were unable to marry her, but Yasmin and RaushenGul had pooh-poohed his hesitation, laughed outrageously at his conformism and he knew better than to resist them.

'Ah the stars,' RaushenGul said looking up at the sky. 'Look at the moon, Poya must be close.'

'Wednesday,' Yusuf muttered noticing that RaushenGul's sari pota had fallen from her head and wondered what his mother-in-law would have to say about that.

'That was a really nice Kaththam, Yasmin aunty,' said Khadeeja.

'Thank you darling! It was so difficult to get hold of Dialog Bhai, he is so much in demand these days.'

'Yeah, nice dinner too,' Saif interjected as he swung himself onto the railing backing the garden .

'So complicated with this man now!' continued Yasmin. 'He has got thoroughly spoilt. You won't believe RaushenGul but he actually told me that if I was not going to have *porichcha koli* in the menu he wasn't going to cook!'

'But the fried chicken was superb aunty!'

'Ah! then good *mawan*. Nice to see the young people interested in the menu and all.' There was a short silence. Then Yasmin began speaking seriously: 'I don't mean to sound insensitive and it's only been seven days since Machaan died…'

'Killed,' RaushenGul interjected.

Yasmin flashed her a look and Yusuf continued '…but one of you must go and see the lawyer and get started on the closure of the estate. These are matters that cannot be rushed and it's best to start dealing with them as early as possible.'

'But we can't do things quickly Yusuf uncle,' Saif said, 'we have to get the police report and the post-mortem report and all those things take time. This is the government we are talking about. Do you know, because it wasn't a natural death we cannot even get a death certificate until we get these reports,' he paused taking time to slide off the railing. 'Actually I had thought about going to see the lawyer earlier but then decided I will go after we get these reports. But if you want, Deeja and I can go and talk to the lawyer tomorrow and just let him know what is happening.'

'Oh! Darling I think that is a good idea,' said Yasmin.

After the children had left the veranda, RaushenGul began to speak. She was nervous and her fingers intertwined obsessively with one another.

'Yasmin, Yusuf machaan, I am worried!'

'Why?' Yusuf queried.

'Because...'

'Yes?' Yusuf persisted puzzled that his normally verbose sister-in-law seemed to be at a loss for words. He had known RaushenGul for a long time and while he sometimes wondered how his *shahalapadi* Rasheed managed with such an opinionated wife he genuinely liked her.

'Yusuf!' Yasmin exclaimed with exasperation. She thought she knew what RaushenGul was getting at and wondered at Yusuf's obtuseness.

'Is it about Khadeeja?' she enquired gently from RaushenGul who nodded blinking back tears.

'It shouldn't be like this. It shouldn't be like this at all but Rasheed goes and dies and now I will have to deal with this all by myself.'

Yusuf was perplexed. Sometimes he felt that women spoke a totally different language.

'*What* about Khadeeja?' he asked impatiently.

'Shush!' Yasmin almost shouted at her husband as she flung a reassuring arm around RaushenGul hugging her close. 'Do you want her to hear? They are just outside they will be able to hear everything.'

'Oh Allah!' RaushenGul moaned, 'What am I to do?'

9

The siblings shuffled out of the veranda and walked towards the stairs.

'Are you tired Dheej?'

'No! In fact I am not sleepy one bit, must have been the coffee! Why?'

'No, just!' said Sabrina and then they all burst out laughing.

'If dad was here he would have a fit if he heard your answer,' said Tariq bringing up the rear.

'Yeah! I can almost hear him say *Just*! What kind of answer is that?'

'It's almost as bad as your mother's nothing.'

They went upstairs talking and laughing amongst themselves and at the landing went towards their own bedrooms.

'Tomorrow then, Dheej,' said Saif as he stood at the entrance of his room.

'Tomorrow what?'

'The lawyer,' said Saif in exasperation. 'You must be tired or in early senility.'

They laughed softly and closed their doors.

Khadeeja looked around her bedroom. She remembered the exact moment when she had moved into her own room. She was fifteen years old. The year had been 1994 and it was a momentous day for her.

The house had been bought by RaushenGul's father, Muhammed Careem in the 1940s when he was a young merchant. It was a large house, located down a lane that bordered a swamp. It sat upfront by the road and the garden sloped down towards the swamp. When it rained, the garden was prone to flood.

When RaushenGul's father moved in, he came with an entourage. In addition to his wife Sara and numerous servants, there were his two younger brothers, one younger unmarried sister, his wife's parents and two of his spinster aunts. By the time children were added to the household the house was bursting at the seams. At one time fifteen people were living under this roof. They decided to move. Flushed with business success, Muhammed Careem bought the house at the corner of the lane - bigger, with more land, and flashier - Venetian chandeliers, stained glass windows and Burma teak carved staircases both back and front. Leaving her father's spinster aunts with her grandparents in the old house, RaushenGul moved with her parents and sister to the new house where she met and then married her cousin Muhammed Rasheed. Her father's wedding gift to her was the original house. It stood emptied of its inhabitants - the grand aunts and grandparents dead. The brothers married and moved into their wives' houses as was tradition. Muhammed Careem's younger sister went to live with his older sister who had married a crockery merchant, lived two houses away and had four sons, one of them Muhammed Rasheed. The old retainers went back to the village and when RaushenGul got married the house lay vacant and abandoned visited only by mosquitoes from the swamp and forsaken cats.

Khadeeja unpacked her bag, sat on the bed, looked at the large antique almirah beside it and her thoughts went back to her very first funeral.

Riyaz Uncle has died and they have just been told that they are to go for his funeral. Khadeeja is seven years old and they are not sure if they understand death.

'It is when you go to sleep and never wake up.' Khadeeja stood with her hands on her hips and surveyed her younger siblings.

'Sabrina, open your eyes.'

'I'm trying to see if I can die.'

'Don't be silly Sabi, just because Khadeeja is the eldest doesn't mean she knows everything. She frequently knows nothing!' Saif teased his eldest sister, 'Death is when you go to heaven. Listen to me, I know. My friend Rohan, his father died last year and he told me that his mother said that his father is with Jesus in heaven.

'Is Riyaz uncle with Jesus in heaven?'

'No stupid! He is with Prophet Muhammed in heaven!'

'I think I want to be with Jesus in his heaven. I like Jesus!' whined Sabrina remembering her Bible stories book.

'My friend told me,' Khadeeja said importantly 'that when your mother dies, your father will marry another woman and she will become your step-mother!'

'Aiyo! That is terrible! What should we do?' Sabrina wrung her hands and looked worried.

'Oh God! Y'all are so stupid. We just must make sure that Mummy does not die!' Khadeeja looked superior and clever.

'I know!' Saif said hitching his trousers up as he bounced onto the bed, 'I have a new game!'

'What? *What*?'

'It's called 'dead'. We have to all fall down dead and not move and not open our eyes and the first one to break the rules is the loser.'

'Children! Are you ready? *What* are you doing?' RaushenGul stood at the door of the bedroom surveying her children fallen on the floor in various grotesque postures with their eyes closed.

'We are playing dead Mummy and Saif is the dead-master and he gives the rules and...'

'Saif! What nonsense is this?' RaushenGul clapped her hands in exasperation. 'No more playing dead. Tariq, my darling, you and Sabrina can't come for the funeral. Both of you have to stay at home with Kusuma. Stop crying now my angel. Mummy will come and give you chocolate cake for tea.'

'Me want come. Me want come,' Tariq wailed unsure as to where the others were going.

'But why can't *I* come? I want to come. It's not fair. I always get left out of everything,' Sabrina added to the fray.

'You are both too young my *ushurus*! Come here, sit on my lap for a moment. Do you remember when Amir uncle died two years ago?' Tariq nodded tearfully as he squashed himself against Sabrina also on RaushenGul's lap.

'See, when Amir uncle died none of you went for the funeral because all of you were too young. But now, Daddy and I think that Saif and Khadeeja are old enough my darling. But you and Sabrina are still a bit too young.'

'Want go next funeral?' Tariq sobbed hopefully. 'Maybe,' replied RaushenGul doubtfully. 'If you are old enough and if you show me that you are a good boy. Next time. Right? Now there is a good boy. *Kusumaaaa*!'

'Sabrina? Are you awake?'

'No! Go to sleep.'

'I am frightened.'

'Why?'

'I had a bad dream.'

'What kind of dream?'

'I dreamt that Ali was wearing sunglasses and he was with Riyaz uncle...'

'Stop! Stooorp! You are making me frightened. I don't want to hear anymore.'

'Let's go and see if Saif is awake.'

'Saif? Saif? Wake up!'

'Hunh! What's happening? What's the matter?'

'Are you frightened?'

'No! Why? Are you both mad? Did you wake me up for this?'

'Because when I close my eyes I see Riyaz uncle wearing sunglasses and he is hiding in the almirah. And he has cotton-wool stuffed up his nostrils!'

'Mummy! Daddy! *Mu-mmm-yeee*!'

10

'*Intestate*? What does that mean?'

Suresh Tambimuttu sat back and surveyed the small delegation before him. He had known them all from childhood, babies really and as soon as he saw them, he realized that he was going to be the bearer of bad news.

'It means that your father did not write a will.'

'What does that mean for us? Will it complicate things?' Saif, who worked in a corporate firm realized that most things seemingly simple became difficult when least expected.

'We-e-ll! It depends.' Suresh was playing for time. As he rubbed his thinning hair he looked at the four young adults before him as if seeing them for the first time. Khadeeja the eldest has grown up to be a voluptuous petite beauty. Funny, he thought, she has RaushenGul's eyes. Almond shaped and light brown, almost golden. Could that be possible? Saif next, how old is he now, almost twenty four, already getting a little pot-belly that boy. And adult acne, must be eating too many chocolates and fast food. Sabrina, tall and slender and serious-looking, more like an older sister even though she is three years younger. Nice haircut, shows off her face. Tariq the baby of them all, he knew was about to enter university in England and was the picture of Muhammed Rasheed when he was young. Even had the same ridiculous hairstyle at the same age. Funny how fashion is cyclical. Bellbottoms, hipsters, long hair, we've all been there, done that. But these youngsters think we were born old. Won't even believe half the things we got up to.

'Does this mean Suresh uncle, that the estate falls under Muslim law?' Khadeeja interrupted Suresh's reverie. She sat on the edge of her chair feeling the sharp edge cut into her thigh. She was beginning to get worried for she had heard that intestate Muslim succession could be notoriously problematic.

'I am afraid so, my dear, and this means that you are better off with a Muslim lawyer than with me. Someone who knows the personal law and deals with it constantly.'

'Can you recommend someone?' Saif asked nervously fiddling with his mobile phone.

'Er… Yes, there is this young chap I met not too long ago. Now what was his name? Rather a personable fellow too. Saif, you may even know him yourself. I think he went to Royal.' Suresh thumbed through his business card holder until he found the name he wanted.

'Ok! Here it is. Let me write it down for you. Jehan Hasan, his offices are down 18th Lane and these are his numbers, both cell and office. I will call him and let him know that you are on the way. Anyway, let me know if you need my help. Talk to me after you talk to him. Ok? I miss your father you know. He was one of the truest friends that I had. Sad! This conflict business. Too many innocent lives lost. Fine man, your father! Fine man!'

Suresh walked the four Rasheed children out of his office and came back to his desk. He had an abstracted expression on his face and as he played with the Tower of London paper weight, he scolded himself. 'Coward! You bloody coward! Now ring up RaushenGul and tell her that you passed the buck. Let's see if you can do *that* like a man.'

As the siblings walked into the bright sunshine Khadeeja raised her head, closed her eyes and sniffed: 'Rain, I smell rain. In about an hour it will rain.'

'Don't be silly Dheej, look at the sky, it is bright sunshine, blue skies, rain - certainly not today.'

'Hey! Saif, have you forgotten that we used to call her The Nose?' Sabrina giggled with Tariq as they shuffled their way down the road looking for a trishaw.

'Hey you two! Knock it off! Just because my nose is somewhat prominent…'

'Prominent! My foot, it is like Air Lanka at lift off. There is that little tip at the end that so looks like an aeroplane…' Saif teased his sister with a wicked gleam in his eye.

'Shuddup! It looks aristocratic or so I have been told by people who appreciate beauty.'

'Appreciate beauty my foot, it is only that half-wit, half-blind Abdullah who appreciates a nose like that. How is he by the way?' Sabrina looked at her sister with an expression that reflected both amusement and concern. 'I am surprised he did not come as well. From all accounts I hear that you two are pasted to one another. Do I hear wedding bells?'

'Oh! Well *he* wants to but I don't know,' said Khadeeja feeling slightly embarrassed. 'Well he is sweet and all that, but now I am not sure. How do you think Mum will take it? Daddy was my buffer for these sorts of things.'

The four of them fell silent as they missed their father. He had been the stable force in their family. They had depended on him to plead their cases throughout their childhood.

'What were you doing?' Rasheed sat sternly in his chair while the three of them stood before him in a straggly line. Saif looked the most frightened and the tears staining Sabrina's plump cheeks indicated that at least one of them had been reduced to tears. Khadeeja alone looked composed and confident. *Always the leader*.

'Making dolls' shampoo Dad.'

'*What*? Ok! Tell me what happened?' He leant forward gravely, his hands intertwined, resting on the desk before him. He felt like a judge and his children seemed suitably awed.

'Well, Sabrina was washing Katy's dress...'

'Katy?'

'...the doll, Dad, the doll,' Sabrina hiccupped.

'Oh! Ok, then what happened?'

'Saif came in and said that he could teach us to make shampoo and then he frothed the water and it became this beautiful green 'cause the colour was running from the dress, but we didn't know it, then Tariq came and said he also wanted to make shampoo and then we took the bottles that our anty-by-otix came in and started filling them and then Saif said that Sabrina was doing it wrong and he grabbed the bottle and then it fell and Tariq started to take the pieces but he didn't know he was doing it wrong and then he...'

'T'wasn't my fault Dad,' Saif interrupted his little face screwed with fear, his eyes pleading. 'Please you have to believe me and Khadeeja says that we have to go to prison and the police will get us and...'

'Okay! Okay! I get the picture.' Rasheed sat back in his chair and surveyed his three children. He was weakly amused but had no intention of letting them see it. He dismissed their fears. 'And what rubbish is all this police nonsense, no-one is going to prison.'

'What has happened Dad? Will Tariq be Ok and why is Mum so mad at us? T'was a assident.' Khadeeja stood calmly before her father, her siblings on either side of her but Rasheed could see turmoil and fear in her eyes too.

She just won't show it, he thought.

'What you all did was not very safe. Mum is right now in hospital with Tariq 'cause he got cut real bad and they are putting stitches into his palm. Khadeeja listen to me. You are the eldest here. You have to take care of the others. You are in charge. I always tell you that you have more responsibility than the others. Tariq got cut badly, if the glass had gone a little bit further the big vein there would have got cut...' Rasheed paused for effect. He looked at his children and then solemnly continued, '...and he could have died.'

Some hours later Tariq accompanied by a grim faced RaushenGul spilled out of the car. As his mother strode sternly into the house his siblings hiding in the side garden loudly whispered to him.

'Hey Tariq! Come here! Let us see the plaster.'

'I's not a plas'er it's a ban'age. The doctor said that I was a brave little boy and that I didn't cry when they sewed me up and that I could have died.'

'The doctor *told* you that?'

'No! But I heard him telling Mum and then Mum began to cry like she normally does and she said that she was going to thrash all of you when she got back home.'

'Omigod! Better scram then before she finds us! Hide the cane! Quick! Break the cane!'

⌒

Holding on to the tuk-tuk as it weaved its way acrobatically through the traffic and turned down 18th Lane, they reached the offices of Jehan Hasan as the rain began to pour down.

'See, I told ya so!' Khadeeja said triumphantly as she opened the door of the office and almost tumbled in followed by her siblings.

11

'Why didn't you tell me before?'

RaushenGul began to cry. The tears poured down swiftly and cleanly. Khadeeja stood before her, her face angry and swollen. RaushenGul knew her well enough to realize she was hurt and bewildered. She tried to comfort her as best as she could, but it was hard.

'Ushuru! Please don't be like this. Daddy and I wanted to tell you but we never found the right time.'

'Right time? Mum don't be ridiculous, I am 25 years old! Dad only just died. Both of you had enough of time to tell me. How long did you think this charade could go on for? I cannot believe that I didn't know about it. How is it possible I ask myself? How come no-one even mentioned it to me?'

'Khadeeja!' RaushenGul sobbed, 'Please don't do this to me. I cannot bear it now. First I lose Dad, I can't bear to lose you!'

'Well, Mum! Shouldn't you have thought of this earlier?'

They were in the study, the only room in the house that was exclusively her father's. RaushenGul sat on the office chair while Khadeeja slouched on a large Indian cushion on the floor. In her hand she held a small packet of letters held together by a rubber band. Suddenly, there were long gaps of silence and she looked around the room. After all these years the space remained unchanged. The room had wall to wall coir matting and was lined with book cupboards from floor to ceiling. The books made it gloomy and dark and you had to turn on the electric light even during the day. In addition to the desk there was a divan on which her father would rest during his afternoon siesta and a low brass table beside it where he kept spectacles while he slept.

RaushenGul lapsed into a long silence and began to look grey and sad. There was an air of forlorn despair. This is my *nasibath*, she thought. Rasheed we did this together… no, that is not true, I did this. But you supported me Rasheed. You were my rock but now you are gone and not only do I not have you but I have to deal with this mess. Oh God! How I miss you! She began sobbing and crying with such intensity that Khadeeja angry and upset though she was, crawled over to her mother and held her hand. Together they wept for their common loss and for the new knowledge gained.

⁀

'Nelum? She knows.'

'Knows?'

'Khadeeja knows.'

'Oh my God, RaushenGul. What are you going to do now?'

Nelum held the phone close to her ear and thought of her friend's predicament. *I knew something awful was going to happen about this. I felt it in my bones.*

'Shall I come there now?'

'I don't know.' RaushenGul was feeling like a boat that had lost its mooring. She knew she would have to talk to her sister Yasmin and her mother about this new development and she was dreading it. They warned me, she thought, they advised me, but Rasheed and I thought we didn't have any need for it. How wrong we were.

Nelum left the receiver with misgiving. She needs me. I must go to her.

Part Two

12

The low country tea estate was broken into three different areas, each one no further than a five minute walk from the other. It had been sold and bought back as the family fortunes dwindled or grew. Mostly sold and rarely bought back, the once majestic, over five hundred acre estate dropped through many generations and was now reduced to a shameful twenty. The house sat on five acres and separated by a road were the other fifteen, which in turn were separated by a medium sized stream into four and eleven acres respectively. Man and Nature had both taken a toll on the once imposing estate which now lay in three pieces like a fragmented Grecian urn.

It was no longer a tea estate exclusively; in fact no-one quite knew what kind of estate it had become. It was experimental with a little forest and a medium sized ayurvedic plantation on one side; with a fruit and vegetable strip and a timber plantation on the other. The house, a badly renovated walauwa sat on top of a very small hill. It overlooked all the lands its owners once possessed, from the paddy fields that fell away below to the neighbouring hills and hillocks that rose up around it.

Arjuna sat on the side veranda with a cold beer. He swilled it straight from the lip of the bottle onto his own. Sitting cross-legged on the hard wooden bench, he drained the whole bottle and continued gazing out at the landscape in front of him. It was late evening and after the quick and quiet sunset he went upstairs to shower and dress for dinner. By the time he came down wearing a red batik sarong and a green T-shirt with his shoulder length hair tied in a low pony tail and still wetly pasted down to the nape of his neck, Swaris had quietly laid the table for dinner. Once Arjuna was seated, Swaris disappeared into the kitchen to re-appear only when he was called by Arjuna.

Arjuna had been living in the house for the past five years. It was he who was responsible for the changing face of the little estate. Yet even though the estate was small, the village remembered that once upon a time his family name was known to them and the next village and the next one. And even though he lived a stripped down sparse version of a landowner's life, the villagers who used to call him Baby *Hamu* then, now called him *Hamu Mahattaya* out of deference to the family reputation and history.

The walauwa had no television. Every evening Swaris locked the rear of the house that contained the kitchen and store rooms, and retired to his own hut positioned slightly away from the walauwa. As the night thickened, Arjuna would sit on the veranda listening to music, smoking a joint or reading a book by the unreliable electric lampshade that stood beside him. As a precaution he would have candles and a box of matches close at hand, as well as a powerful torch. One never knew when the power would go out or if it would return anytime soon. He retired early. He needed to in order to be up at four every morning. These days, sleep generally came easy.

It was different before. There was a time in his life he would stay up until two o'clock in the morning courting sleep. Reading, pacing, smoking and finally, in desperation, popping sleeping pills hoping it would let him rest. Here, no sooner did he lie down in bed he would fall asleep to the sound of cicadas' chirping and Balla barking at an errant mouse that had dared trespass on his territory. Life was different now. He had achieved a controlled peace of mind. Not too much thought; the only books he allowed himself to read were those on agriculture, not too much distraction, not too much drink, not too much talk. At times he would ask himself if it was a life but he knew where he had been before and what he had lived through. For now, this was enough. It was more than enough. He was content.

'Here. Drop me off here.' Khadeeja leant forward and tapped the van driver on the shoulder.

'But miss, I can take you right to the house. We can ask for directions in town. They are sure to know of it.'

'No, drop me off here. I have to buy a few supplies.' She climbed down from the van and hoisted her bags on her shoulder.

'Shall I wait for you miss? *Karadarayak Na.* No problem.' The van driver was concerned about his mostly silent, young female passenger. She hadn't engaged him in conversation during the five hour journey and spent most of her time gazing far out into the distance or scribbling furiously into her notebook. She must be having problems, he thought. *Laoow*. Its always *laoow* with these pretty girls. Then sighed. Don't we all?

'No. That's ok. I know where the house is, it's not far. I can make it from here. *Bohoma Isthuthi*. Thank you very much. You better leave for Colombo right away so that you can get there before dark. Here's the money.'

'Thank you very much Miss. *Deviyangé pihitay*.' God Bless! He let the clutch out and careened down the road blasting his horn at unwary pedestrians.

Khadeeja looked after the van for a few seconds, then ran her fingers through her hair, shouldered her knapsack and trudged towards the vegetable seller at the corner.

'Where can I find a place to stay in this town?'

'Hmm,' the man replied in Sinhala, as he scratched his head and screwed his eyes in thought. 'Tchah! There are not many places to stay here. Why don't you try the next town five miles away? It's a pity you sent your driver away. The next bus will take about twenty minutes to come.'

'No!' she said sharply. 'I want to stay here, in this town.'

The vegetable seller hoisted his sarong and stood up. He surveyed the dusty narrow road before him and upon catching sight of a plump, prosperous looking man shouted out to him 'Oy! Sudu Mahattaya! This Miss needs a place to stay.'

The owner of the only wine store, 'Ever Flourish Wine and Beer Shop', which was really a small cupboard with a grill in front that sold mostly arrack, gave the young woman a quick look. He took his time folding his sarong neatly and knotting it at his waist showing his sturdy, hairy calves and came down the steep steps towards her.

'What can I do for you miss?' he asked in a husky voice edging closer to the young woman.

Khadeeja adjusted her bags on her shoulder and shrank slightly 'I need a place to stay tonight. I was told that there was a house that gives out rooms. Do you know where that is?'

'Ah! Yes, why not. She is speaking of Hamu Mahattaya's place. Don't you remember Nimal, our Hamu Mahattaya has become the town inn-keeper these days.' He giggled wheezily at the vegetable seller who looked embarrassed and busied himself tucking his sarong into his thighs allowing a large obscene pouch to gather between his legs.

13

The ROOMS TO RENT cardboard sign hung lopsided on the gate. As Khadeeja walked down the driveway and tolled the large temple bell that hung from a nearby mango tree, she looked around the neatly tended garden for someone to appear. She heard a sound and looked up. A middle aged man with betel stained teeth materialised, looked at her and went back into the house. Then, a younger man came out wearing a pair of shorts, and a torn T-shirt. He carried a soiled gardening fork and his bare feet made a muddy pattern on the cement floor. She was taken aback when he spoke to her in English. She noticed that the first man still hovered in the background.

'Yes?' the second man said a trifle impatiently and on hearing her query was surprised that she wanted to stay there.

'We normally only get foreigners for short periods of time, two, three days. Not like how you want, for three weeks. This estate is in the middle of nowhere, what for coming here? There is nothing of interest to see, so it's used for stopovers generally, if you know what I mean. So now tell me, what are you going to be doing here?'

She was prepared for the onslaught of questions and so introduced herself as a social anthropologist studying the housing conditions of the tea-pluckers.

'I have actually finished much of my research,' she said. 'I just need a quiet place to do the writing.'

Arjuna broke into a reluctant smile, his light brown eyes lighting up, 'Well, actually it's a good thing that my tea-pluckers will not be harassed by you; in any case this is a *punchi watte*, a small estate, I only have day labourers. Now, let me see,' he drummed his fingers on the side table as he thought. 'You will want to see a room, no? And I can give you all three meals if you want. That is no trouble. Now one bedroom has an attached bathroom. It's clean and all that but not very hi-fi if you know what I mean; the other bedroom is much better but if you take it you will have to use the bathroom at the end of the hall.' He spoke while ushering her into the house.

She shrugged her backpack off her shoulders and entered. They both casually wandered towards the bedrooms, he lifted a curtain and revealed sparse functional rooms for her to choose from. In the end she chose the nicer bedroom without the attached bathroom. It had French windows on the right that opened out onto the side veranda and onto a private enclosed garden on the left. The garden had a shower tied to the trunk of a coconut tree, which she could use when the weather was good. It had a murky pond and an araliya tree that shed its flowers constantly so that the grass had a carpet of araliya flowers.

The high wooden ceiling was carved intricately and the four poster bed sat solidly in the middle of the room.

'I'll take this,' she said and smiled for the first time at Arjuna. 'By the way my name is Deeja.'

'Arjuna,' he said as he nodded and went off to get her a cup of tea.

14

It was now almost one week since Deeja was at the estate. She woke late, had a breakfast of fruit from the back garden, went for long walks and on particularly hot days she knotted a *diya redde* below her small protruding belly, wore a T-shirt over her bikini top, and bathed at the spout at the bottom of the land. The area was spectacularly beautiful. It lay in a valley ringed with black mountains that stretched high into the blue sky. Some, she thought, as she swung lazily in the crudely made hammock of rope, may feel claustrophobic. She lay on her back and watched an eagle swoop and soar, joined by one then another, and another. They seemed to float from one end of the sky to the other, carried by the wind, creating a ballet of movement.

Arjuna's day began early. Once he left the house she didn't see him until dinner. She had a solitary lunch of red rice and curry, it was paid for after all and in a short space of time each had fallen into a pattern of life that they seemed comfortable with.

She tried to keep up the pretence of being there on work and made sure she took her laptop with her but instead she began keeping a diary of sorts, recording thoughts and feelings that overtook her during her solitary moments.

'Good day?'

'Yeah! A few labour problems but other than that yes, not a bad day.'

They were seated on a rock at the top of the property watching the sunset clothe the land in orange and gold. 'Sometimes when it's a really clear day, you can see all the way down to Dondra.'

'In the old days, apparently you could see Adam's Peak from Colombo.'

'Today, you can't even see the end of the road due to the pollution. We are going to ruin this country.'

'Going to?' One eyebrow raised, head at an angle. Hair tousled by the wind.

'Yeah! You are right, it's already done. These bloody mad dog politicians!'

'How pessimistic we are,' Deeja commented. 'It must be our generation, the pes-gen.'

Arjuna grinned. 'D'ya have plans for the weekend? I'm off on Saturday so if you want I can take you on my bike and we can check out some of the nearby areas. So, what d'ya say?'

'Very much. Thanks!' Deeja looked at him her eyes narrowing in the glare of the setting sun.

That night Deeja lay sleepless hearing the grandfather clock strike eleven, midnight, one o'clock. She got out of bed, walked towards the side veranda and into the garden. The poya moon was bright and incandescent. Crickets chirped and somewhere a lone nightingale sang a song of love. She craned her neck and looked at the shadow on the moon and remembered the bedtime story her father used to relate to them.

Once upon a time, in the empire of the rising sun, there lived a little rabbit who made the best rice cakes in the land. People came from far and wide to eat his rice cakes. One day, when the rabbit was wandering through the forest he came upon magnificently dressed samurai practicing their skills. The rabbit fell in love! 'I want to be a samurai,' he said to the villagers who came to buy his rice cakes. 'Nonsense!' They laughed at him. 'Rabbits cannot be samurai!' The rabbit was disheartened and continued making rice cakes but yearned secretly to become a samurai. One day, as luck would have it, an old samurai warrior made a deal with the rabbit that he would impart his fighting skills to the rabbit in exchange for an endless supply of rice cakes during the apprenticeship. At the end of six months of rigorous training, the rabbit was as skilled as a fully fledged samurai. 'Of course,' the old samurai warrior said, 'no rabbit can ever become a samurai, the only place you could pass off as one is at the annual competition hosted by the emperor. Enter the games dressed in full samurai gear, but on no account are you to remove your helmet and show who you are!' So with the help of his old master, the rabbit pinned down his long ears, wore a helmet, tied a sash around his belly and rode off towards the capital. 'Don't forget,' the old warrior shouted after the rabbit; 'never remove your helmet, whatever happens.' At the games, the rabbit trounced all he competed against. His jump and his dexterity had him defeating all comers and he won the affection of the crowd. 'Who is this wonderful warrior?' the crowd asked, and begged him to reveal himself. The rabbit refused. But eventually even the emperor asked to see who this new and dazzling warrior was. 'Remove your helmet,' the emperor commanded in admiration, 'you may join the ranks of my samurai.' Rabbit was forced to obey. He took off the helmet and out popped two long ears! The crowd turned angry. The rice-cake rabbit is making fun of us and our traditions they said. Oh dear! thought the emperor, we cannot have a samurai rabbit, that just will not do. 'What else can you do dear rabbit?' he asked. 'I make the best rice cakes in the whole land, your Highness,' came the reply. And so the emperor who loved rice cakes came up with a solution. He said that his empire extended up to a dark and lonely satellite called the moon, which he was obliged to visit. Could the wonderful samurai rabbit go there and make rice cakes for him? And so it happens that as soon as the entire moon is full and bulging white with rice cakes, the emperor visits the rabbit and for fourteen days he steadily eats the delicious rice cakes. When they are all eaten, the emperor leaves and the rabbit begins again to make rice cakes for the emperor's next visit. Even today, if you look up at the moon, you can see the rabbit busily making rice cakes.

'Cool story.'

'Yes!' Khadeeja agreed, 'My dad used to tell us stories to make us go to sleep.' She felt a wave of sadness overtake her.

'So, is it working?'

'I think it is. We have an early start tomorrow, it might be a good idea if I head off to bed now.' She gathered her slippers and headed towards her room. At the door she turned back to look at Arjuna. He saw her and raised a hand in salute. She smiled, even though she knew he wouldn't be able to see it and closed her door. As she began drifting into sleep she recollected walking in the gardens and catching a small movement from the corner of her eye. Arjuna was seated on a stone, smoking and watching her gravely.

'You too?' she had asked.

'What?'

'Couldn't sleep.'

He nodded and she stood for a moment awkwardly waiting, wondering if she should go back to her room or if she should join him. Then she saw him move over and make room on the stone for her.

15

The next day as they roared up the mountain road feeling the wind nip their cheeks, Khadeeja clutched onto Arjuna's waist and for the first time in many days, felt happy. They had taken a packed lunch of chicken roast, kadé paan, pol sambol and beer. 'Swaris is hopeless in the kitchen department,' Arjuna sheepishly apologised as Khadeeja's eyes twinkled while they packed the food in neat little parcels. 'Food's not important for me, Pol sambol and bread is a feast fit for a king, I say,' she reassured him as they took extra care to pack some chilled beers in a cold bag.

'Where are you taking me?'

'I'll tell you what? Keep quiet now and in a *chooti* bit you'll see soon enough. Just remember to bring your bathers.'

The motorcycle roared through the narrow roads, curving downward to take the bends in one beautiful sweep. The wind blew through their hair and flung their words out into the landscape filling their ears with currents of air.

The countryside wore a dress of green and white – tea bushes and waterfalls. A delicate sweep of rolling hills that gave way to the great rain forest Sinharaja beyond.

They were headed for the Tangamale Plains, a remote area of un-describable loveliness. Once there, Arjuna hurled his knapsack to the ground by the small waterfall and began to strip down to his swimsuit worn under his jeans.

'Come on men!' he urged Deeja as he dived straight into the ice cold rock pool. He gave shrieks and gasps as his body hit the freezing water making her wince at the thought of following him in. First dipping her toes, then her foot, then her calves Deeja was in the process of slow torture of her body when suddenly Arjuna hurled himself at her, wrapped his arms around her knees and brought her crashing into the water. Yelling and swearing, Deeja spluttered curses at her tormentor pushing him away with force as Arjuna still clutched on to her. A second later realizing their close proximity, embarrassed at their spontaneous reactions, they finished their dip with more respectability and restraint.

⌒

By the end of the second week they began to speak about his wife.

'Where is she?' Deeja asked and he knew exactly whom she meant.

'She's gone home for a visit. She is German.'

'German!' A little higher and her voice would have gone through the roof. 'How did you meet a German?'

It put him on the defensive, this line of questioning, as if he had no right to be married, as if he had no right to be married to an European. He wasn't sure if he wanted to go into the whole thing with her. It was too tiresome, all those explanations of situations even he wasn't very sure of. He ignored her question and she didn't push.

Then another time he said as Swaris served them Spaghetti Bolognese, 'Christine taught Swaris how to make this. Christine, my wife,' he added quickly.

'How global,' she replied, 'a German teaching a Sri Lankan how to cook Italian.' Then she wished she hadn't said it in that manner. 'It's very nice,' she said quickly but knew that he had got hurt.

⌒

'Isn't it strange how men don't have the need to be surrounded by family photographs?'

'What d'ya mean?' he asked absently. They had finished their afternoon lunch and sat together on the wooden bench on the side veranda. He was hunched slightly forward looking down towards the paddy fields and she was seated with her knees up and feet placed on the seat of the bench.

They were both smoking cigarettes. Or rather Arjuna was and Khadeeja just waved her cigarette about, gesticulating, using it as a prop to make a point, to fill a silence, to move her hands. She was not a smoker but liked the idea of it. She was never sure if she was doing it right, but it did not matter. She liked the ritual of lighting the cigarette, placing it in her mouth, drawing a breath in, taking the cigarette out, holding the breath, and then slowly, slowly blowing a cloud of smoke out. She liked the feel of silent companionship; she liked the camaraderie that was built between them. It made her feel closer to him.

'If you look at men's houses or apartments they rarely have photographs of their families plastered all over. I mean look at this house. There is nothing here. No photograph of even your poor balla. But women, however, I must clarify that my knowledge is mostly of American women, seem to carry and have photographs everywhere. They even have photographs in their offices. Sometimes I would get sick of having to sit through the reams and reams of photographs the women pull out of their wallets, of their children, of their husbands, of their boyfriends, of their dogs. Yes!' she chuckled, 'of their dogs as well.'

'I grew up,' he said, 'in a house that had no photos. It wasn't my father's rule. It was my mother's. So my dear woman, it's not only men who don't have photographs. Photos are a way of remembering, if you know what I mean. Sometimes it is better not to remember. Photographs are history. Sometimes you have no history. Or no history worth remembering.' He twisted his head towards her and a bitter smile hung on his lips.

Does he know, she suddenly thought. *My God, he knows!* She felt her heart beat faster realizing she had not expected this.

That evening while she read in her room with both sets of French windows open to the elements, she found him standing just inside her room holding a photograph.

'Here! I thought you might like to see what the wife looks like,' he said. In the picture a woman stood on a beach wearing a black bikini, her arms around a child. She was tanned and her blond hair was tied back in a ponytail. She wasn't smiling and had an air of gravity about her.

'Who is the child?'

'Oh! Some local kiddo she made friends with.'

'How did you meet?'

'I met her in Hix... Hikkaduwa. I was working there in one of the hotels and she had come on a holiday. She was being pestered one day by these beach touts and I just happened to come along and rescue her. The rest is history. Ya know like a fairy tale and real romantic and all.' he smiled a wry smile. 'We had a long distance relationship for a few years and then we decided to get married.'

'Your family?' There she said it, now she knew there would be no turning back. 'So what did your family say?'

'What could they say? Nothing! They politely came for the small wedding, ate the cake, shook hands and buggered off as fast as possible. I am not *thada* with them. Barely on hi-bye terms actually. We have had problems in the past, but now we have a happy medium. They don't care about me and I don't care about them.' He laughed and said, 'Not everyone has a fairy tale life.'

16

I am confused. She is messing up my head but yet I don't want to tell her to go away, to mind her own business. All those questions she has. What a lot of questions for such a small girl. She wants to know everything almost like she wants to memorize my life. Now she asks about Christine. But I am not ready to tell her. Not yet...

I met Christine eight years ago. I was working at the front desk at the Hotel Hikkaduwa. I had just ditched Colombo. Couldn't really continue staying at home you know.

Things over there were getting really bad. *Maara* bad you know. If I didn't leave at that point the secret would have become a *kachchaal* and I knew that my mother, she just wouldn't have been able to deal with it. She *needed* it to be a secret. For her it was a *maara* secret that could not be spoken about. That is the way with our people, you know. This is the way they deal with these things. So, I split and she knew that I did it for her. She came with me to the Pettah bus stand and at that time we didn't know where I would be going. Earlier she said that maybe I should go to some relative's place in the hills. But I didn't want to deal with relatives or them casting remarks or those *chusfying* whispers and 'in vain' kind of looks behind my back. I wanted to go to a place where no-one would know me, where I could sit and think and decide what to do with my life.

You know, it's easier if you have had nothing at all from the beginning. You have no illusions, no dreams. You just think of surviving. Of taking one step at a time. But when you have led a cushy life, had a roof over your head, food on the table, clothes on your back, you get soft. You lose your edge for survival. Every little knock seems to be a crisis. In a way, in retrospect, I am glad I left home. This is real life. This is the truth.

The first intercity bus out of the depot was bound for Hikkaduwa. I took it. Apoi! It was terrible. A godawful trip. All those smells, the blaring radio, the jerking motion. I nearly catted and eventually after three miserable hours, for my luck I got dropped off in front of one of the big hotels. I knew I had to sort myself out quickly. I didn't have much dough. Just before I left my mother thrust a neatly folded small envelope into my hand. 'You don't have to…' I began, not making any effort to return it. She just shook her head and her eyes glistened. She closed her hand over mine and said 'I wish I had more, but this is all I have.' In the bus I opened the envelope and discovered five thousand bucks. There was a note which I crushed and threw out of the window without even reading.

I needed a place to crash out, so I walked into the first clean looking hotel I saw and asked to see the manager. I told him a half truth, family problems, needed some work. I was lucky I spoke the *kaduwa* well. That is the ticket these days. At least I am grateful *they* sent me to Elocution class. So with my English language skills and good karma I suppose, I got a job as a receptionist, a small room in the staff quarters, three meals a day, Monday's off and a small salary. If I worked well and they were happy with me I had a future here at the hotel they told me. 'Why Mr. Gunasekera you could even become the general manager here one day.' I smiled and thanked them. But I knew I wasn't going to hang about for long.

How did I meet on Christine? I was friendly with all the guests, most of them were German, some Italians, some French. I had the night shift and sometimes when they couldn't sleep or if they were lonely they would come down and hang out in the lobby. Then they would start chattering. Some of them didn't know any English and soon I had a smattering of French, German, Italian, even a bit of Japanese. *Konichiwa*! The waiters and beach touts were better than I was. They had the language deal down pat. *Bonjour! Guten Morgan! Ciao! Arigato!* For them it was a matter of making a buck. Money is a big incentive to learn anything.

Our guests were the package holiday lot. Factory workers, janitors, bus drivers and secretaries. This was no five star hotel that catered to the select. This was get by with doing the minimum. Most of them had saved the entire year to come here. They had worked through summers and skimped and saved to visit paradise. Every year they would go somewhere different. Always package tours, mostly to places that were warm.

All of them seduced by the sun and sand. This time it was Sri Lanka, next year it would be Thailand. Cheap holidays with cheap food and good service. They came by the planeloads, were carted onto tour buses and straight from the airport driven for two and a half or three hours to the hotel. There they were settled in and we took over.

It was all so easy when you thought about it. Get a bunch of white people to buy the idea of an ideal holiday of sun, sea and sand. Give them a *yakko* welcome drink with an orchid stuck on the side, give them lots of badly cooked pasta and meat for dinner, have plenty of deck chairs out on the beach and by the pool, every evening hire a few inept village dancers who will twirl and whirl out a made-up devil dance, clinched with home made costumes. Serenade them with a three piece travelling calypso band complete with straw hats and a limited repertoire. After two weeks, they leave lobster red and sunburnt and the new lot arrive for the whole song and dance to be played out again. The tour agencies and hotels had it down pat. What the holidaymakers were not told about were the beach touts who hounded you, the beggar children who followed you, the shop keepers who ripped you off, the young men who touched your bottom, and the young boys forced into prostitution to 'entertain' you.

⌒

Early one morning, after work, while on a long walk on the beach I saw a woman being harassed by some young *thraada* looking boys. When they see a white woman they have an antenna only for one thing. Anyway, this poor girl was wearing a bikini swimsuit with a cover-up. There were about four of them and they were pulling at her straps and trying to take her cover-up off. They were touching her face and trying to feel her breasts. It was horrifying to watch. So I yelled and started running towards them.

Palayang, I shouted, leave her alone. They ignored me, after all I was just one man and they were four. The woman didn't know what was happening, she kept beating their hands off and saying *Nein*! *Nein*! Then she sat down on the beach. When I got close to them, the beach boys recognized me and they smiled and said *Karadarayak naa mahattaya. May suddi nikang kaagahanawa*. We don't need white flesh they said and thrashed off into the shrub. I bent down towards the woman; she was still seated passively on the sand. I held out a hand to help her up and she took it silently and brushed the sand off herself. She didn't utter one word, but tears were pouring down her cheeks while we walked back towards the hotel. She was one of our guests.

The next day the manager called me and said that one of the guests had mentioned that I was to be given a small gift for coming to her aid.

'Mr Arjuna,' he said, 'there is one Miss Klaus who is wanting to make a small, small presentation.'

There stood Christine unsmiling and quite solemn. She was wearing a pareo and a short cropped t-shirt. She was with bare feet and her blond hair was tied back into a ponytail. She looked as if in her late twenties. She held out an envelope and even though I protested and said that I hadn't done it to get anything and it was the decent thing to do and that these beach boys are a menace to society, you could see that the management just wanted this over and done with. 'Ha right! Mr Arjuna. Ok! Ok, now no? Happy no? All we wants is our guests to be happy. Isn't that right Mr Arjuna? He and we thanks you Miss Klaus,' and he bowed and scraped us both out of his presence.

So I took the envelope, thanked her and walked back to my quarters. I sat heavily on the bed and opened the envelope. And Machaan! What a presentation! At first I couldn't believe it. I counted it over and over again. The woman had given me a thousand dollars. A fucking thousand dollars! Machaan! I was laughing! So what did I do? I'm not a fool! Ok, so maybe there was a flash of a sec when I thought that maybe I should have been more grateful. Go back to her, *ambarannafy* a bit, tell her it was too much, make her feel good etc, etc. But hey! She must be earning this in a month. Maybe even more. This is chicken feed to them suddas.

I kept the dough, even slept that first night with my right hand under the pillow on top of the cash.

Sometimes details are not important. Who said what and where and when? Who did what and where and how? The details don't matter because the consequences are more important. At the end of her holiday Christine didn't go back. She stayed on to be with me. We began having a relationship of sorts. Christine, I discovered was twenty-nine years old and a physiotherapist. After she had been with me for a month I left the hotel. It was becoming a *karadaré* for both the management and me to remain in their employment. To tell you the truth, it was not unusual for employees to shag the guests. It happened all the time. You would hear of the waiters boasting of how this *baduwa* or that was making the moves on them. They were usually older women, it was the older women who were the easiest. Sri Lankan men knew how to sweet talk. It just didn't bother them if the woman was married or old or fat or had her children with her. All women were fair game. How many women could you bed? That was the ultimate goal. And the women, I don't know if they got caught up in the holiday romance idea. Whether they thought it would lead to something. But almost always the romances were for something the men could get out of the women, either money or sex, most times it was for both.

I remember one of the waiters boasting about how he had done a guest while her husband was dead to the world on the other bed. He had met her at the hotel disco and while employees are not supposed to fraternise with the guests it does happen. So he had met up with her and she told him to come up to her room. When he went there, he saw a man sleeping on the other bed, He tried to leave, but she said don't worry he won't wake up. The waiter stayed. The husband slept. And the next day the whole hotel was buzzing with the exploit.

Some of the waiters would sleep with the male guests, I can't say that they were *ponnayas*, I know they didn't think of it that way. They said they did it for the money, the presents, the free ticket once a year to Germany or Switzerland or wherever the men came from. Soon even we would kid them. 301 has a big basket, Pradeep, we would say as we passed him knowing that Pradeep would turn round and look at the man's crotch. Sometimes when we wanted to be nasty we would call them pillow biters in front of everybody. Just like that! But most times it was not the waiters these men were after, it was the boys. Everybody knew about that, even the police but no-one cared a damn! Every so often they would do a raid, make a few arrests, splash it in the papers and in two days you would see the men walking free, one arm around another young boy and the other hand giving high five's to their friends.

Anyway, the hotel would turn a blind eye to all this. Our guests come first. It's not our business what they do or what they want, or why they come to our country. It's not our concern if they want a one night stand or a long term relationship, if they want a boy or a girl or a duck or a fish! It's not our problem.

But Christine was no one night stand and they knew it. She began hanging out in my quarters and while we could move in and out of the guests lives it was quite another thing for a guest to enter our lives. The other boys were just not cool with Christine being around and the management began making comments, so we moved out.

We found a small annexe with one bedroom and a toilet that had been added on at the back. It had no drawing room but the veranda in front was large enough to have two chairs and a small coffee table. It was painted green.

⌒

No. I can't say I was in love with Christine then. I think I fell into a situation. Christine said she was in love with me. She accepted all the conditions I laid out. I told her that I had no money, I told her about falling out with my parents, that I couldn't go crawling back to them and she understood. You have to give it to these *suddas*, they don't wait hanging around for Mama and Papa. They know how to live life on their terms. Make it or break it.

I have a little bit of money she said, don't worry about that and later if it comes to it we could go back to Germany together. What will we do for now? I asked. Travel she said, I always hated these package trips, now we can travel all over the country. Just you and I.

And off we went. The length and breadth of where we could go. The sunrise at Pottuvil, the sunsets at Kalpitiya, the Yala leopards, the Nilaweli beach, the Anuradhapura temples, the Sigiriya frescoes, the Polonnaruwa ruins, the Kandy perehara, the Nuwara Eliya races, the Galle fort, the Rekewa turtles, the Uda Walawe elephants...

I told her stories of the places we couldn't go to. Places that when I was a child did not belong to the conflict areas, places that appeared peaceful. But now of course we know better.

⌒

When I want to remember Christine I close my eyes and take a deep breath. My first memory of Christine is of her smell. At first I couldn't place it and it began to bug the hell out of me. It was all over her - her mouth, her hair, her hands, her skin. One day as we walked by the beach not touching and yet walking so close that our arms swung into one another, it came to me.

Suduru. 'Cumin!' I exclaimed aloud. 'You smell of sweet cumin.'

'Ja!,' she smiled pleased, 'I do. My perfume is cumin-based.'

'Come again,' I said, 'I have never heard of such a thing.'

'I make it.'

Christine was first acquainted with cumin as a child. When baking bread in their rural farm house on the outskirts of Karlsruhe, just before popping it into the oven, her mother would rub ground sweet cumin all over the dough. 'Christine,' her mother would say, 'remember, smell is everything. With a smell you can have a man, with a smell you can make potatoes become meat.' Their hands intertwined with the dough, Christine clutched at her mother's calloused reddened palms within the soothing coolness of the dough. 'Christine, remember,' her mother would say, 'be a somebody in life, don't settle for being a nobody. Don't be like me Christine, don't be like me.' At night while she burrowed deep into the covers and blocked out the sound of her parents arguing, she would smell her hands and take deep breaths of sweet cumin and feel comforted.

After eight months, Christine said she needed to go back to Germany to sort out her affairs. She stayed away for a year, sent me money every month. We had this dream together, Christine and I, we wanted to have a piece of land of our own where we would grow our own food and be self-sufficient. You know do the eco-friendly thing before it became fashionable even. But *wattes* don't grow on trees, they take money to buy and I was having a hard time finding another job. Then her grandmother died and left her a little bit of money and that's when she came back here and we got married.

Why did we get married? That is a difficult question. I could have gone on quite happily without it. But Christine seemed to need it. It's funny how similar situations can have different reactions in people. We both had unhappy childhoods and while I shunned family or anything closely resembling it, Christine craved it. She wanted a house, children, the family dog.

When she first came back, every so often she would bring the subject up. It became like drops of water on a stone. Every day a question would drop on the stone. Every day the stone became more smooth, more worn down, more concave. Then one day, I thought why not? I had no family - no real family to speak of. Christine was good to me. She cared for me. She loved me. No-one had loved me before for who I was. She gave me a home.

I told her...

17

...King Arjuna was never to know who had been responsible for the transformation of the Arjuna Gardens as they were now called. His kingdom became known far and wide for its magnificent landscapes, his people stopped talking of overthrowing him, and the keeper of the forest remained a young girl through the years. After many, many years, long after the king had died the people forgot his name, they forgot the name of the gardens and one day they began to call it...

'... the Garden of Five Senses,' Deeja finished his sentence for him.

'You know *that* story,' he said, 'that story was told to me by my Sheila Ayah. When I came here I thought like my namesake King Arjuna, I too would like to have a Garden of Five Senses. And so I began to build it, to shape it, to create an Arjuna Garden.'

'What does Christine say about the Gardens?'

'She loves them. In fact she gave me the idea for this garden. After I had finished the other four it was this one that gave me the most amount of *vathey*. The garden of Touch. I didn't know what to do with it. The others were easy but how the hell do you depict touch. I would come here for hours when the land had been cleared and sit on this rock and wonder what the hell to do with it. One day, Christine found me asleep and she woke me by stroking my face with a blade of grass. And then *patas* I got it. I knew what to do. Out here in the village they say that grass has a healing touch. In fact when a child is just beginning to walk, they make it walk on grass. No slippers, no shoes, just grass.'

They lay flat on the grass side by side, their arms stretched out, their legs slightly akimbo. An aquamarine blue sky shimmered and shone above them.

'You know, every afternoon Sheila Ayah would take a *padura* to the garden and lay it below the jumbu tree. She would place me on her outstretched legs with my head on her feet. She would then begin to rock me, gently at first and if I hadn't fallen asleep after half an hour she would shake me violently from side to side as if to chase the wakefulness out of me. It generally worked. In no time I would fall asleep. She would always tell me a story as I lay on her legs watching the branches wave in the air, seeing patches of blue through green.'

'This is such a peaceful place,' Deeja murmured.

They conversed with their eyes closed. It was easier that way, the hazy sunshine hurt their eyes and by closing them they were aware of their surroundings even more.

'I wish I had an estate. My parents were obsessed with selling land rather than acquiring it,' Deeja smiled as she said. It was a constant disagreement that she had with her parents who couldn't forget the era of consumer protectionism and land requisition that lost them most of their lands and forced all citizens to live frugal lives. In contrast Deeja found her generation excessive spenders, risk-takers and aggressive business people almost as if it were an instinctive reaction to the impositions of yester-year.

'This is not my *watte*. It is Christine's,' Arjuna was quiet in his admission.

'What do you mean Christine's? Did she create all of it?'

'No, it means that Christine *owns* it.' Arjuna looked at her, his light brown eyes serious and yet there was an air of forced light-heartedness about him. There was a resolution that she had not seen in him before. Later she would think of this time as the beginning of his unburdening.

'But that is not possible Arjuna, these are your estates. Your family has owned them for centuries. You have lived here all these years.'

'How do you know that?'

Deeja thought quickly. 'You told me a few days ago.'

'Did I?' Arjuna seemed suspicious.

'Of course you did Arjuna, or else, how would I know these things? We were in the gardens and you mentioned it. Anyway, go on with what you were saying.'

'So where was I? Oh! Right,' he said distractedly, 'I have been able to live here all these years because of Christine. It's complicated Deeja. If you think other people's lives are an *achchaaru* then mine is more so. After Christine and I had finished travelling, I went to my mother and asked her if I could live on her *watte* with Christine. My mother agreed but the others in the family like my father and my aunts were totally against it but maybe they thought it kept me out of their way. The family didn't give us anything. I know my mother would have wanted to give me more but in the end she was too weak and allowed herself to be bullied by the others. Nothing but the permission to live on the land was given. So, I was allowed to take care of the *watte* but would be paid no salary and they wanted me to know it was never to be mine. You could say that I was a *hamu murakaraya*. A gentleman watcher.

Then, through a distant cousin, a real gossip *haminé*, we came to know that the *watte* had been quietly put on the market. I went down to Colombo and slammed my mother with the information and she confirmed it. Some debts had come up suddenly and my father pressured my mother to sell the *watte*. 'What can I do Arjuna putha?' my mother said. 'When he makes his mind up there is no changing it.' Then Christine suggested we buy it, so, on the sly we put an offer through a friend. My father didn't know it was Christine buying it or else it would have been hat and he wouldn't have allowed my mother to sell it to her. It must just annoy the hell out of them to know that now we live here legitimately and this is ours.' His story finished, Arjuna rested back on his outstretched palms and closed his eyes wearily.

Khadeeja sat up and looked at him confused. 'But why did you want to own this estate in the first place? If I had the money to buy land I certainly wouldn't buy land which is grudged, if you know what I mean. You said you don't get on too well with your family, right? So if it were me, I would buy land far, far away from any family property. Start afresh, cut the umbilical cord.' Deeja knew she was baiting him but she couldn't help it. She wanted to know how much he knew, and if he would confide in her.

'Today, you ask me that question, and I don't know the answer. At that time, it seemed the best thing to do. We had spent some time already in this place, we had worked like dogs on it and created a paradise for the two of us. Somehow, to us it seemed like our land. We loved it and we felt that we belonged here. I don't know maybe it's a stupid sentimental answer. Maybe I am a stupid sentimental being. Also,' he laughed, 'the price was very low.' He smiled and shrugged indifferently and busied himself with changing the CD, in the boom box. Deeja settled herself onto the mat and rested her head on a pillow. They lit up a joint, poured out two arracks and soda and were suddenly quiet and withdrawn, drawing on the roach, passing it back and forth, letting Pink Floyd seep into them and fill the air.

There is no pain, you are receding.
A distant ship smokes on the horizon.
You are only coming through in waves.
Your lips move but I can't hear what you're saying.
When I was a child I had a fever.
My hands felt just like two balloons.
Now I got that feeling once again.
I can't explain, you would not understand.
This is not how I am.
I have become comfortably numb.

'It's going to rain,' she said looking up at the cloudless sky.

'Yes! Around midnight.' Arjuna agreed and then, 'How do *you* know? There isn't a cloud in the sky.'

'I don't know, I just know.'

'Me too!' He shrugged, they smiled and Deeja was more pleased than he would ever guess.

'There is nothing to beat Pink Floyd when you are getting stoned.'

She turned towards him to answer, almost reached out and touched him and as she looked at Arjuna seated beside her looking at her, suddenly thought to herself; *Don't* and then *Can't*.

18

The next morning Deeja woke up late. She felt rested and fresh and as she stretched her limbs awake, she saw a cloud scudding across the blue sky and heard the twitter and chirps of house sparrows and realized that she had slept the night outside on the mat. Nothing like sleeping on Mother Nature's own floor for your back, she thought as she padded towards her bedroom. The house was deserted. Arjuna must have left for work; she gathered her clothes and headed for the bathroom.

Mid-morning as she worked on her computer in the dining room, she saw a hand leave a glass of *thambili* at the edge of the table.

'Thanks Swaris,' she said automatically reaching for it and taking a sip.

'At least take the trouble to remember my name,' said Arjuna's voice and she started up in surprise to see him silhouetted against the window backing the light, his wet hair sleek and polished.

'Oh sorry! I didn't expect to see you here, I thought you were at work.'

'What work? After last night, I feel like hell! I must have passed out on the mat and all that talk about sleeping on the floor is good for the body is jackshit! I am suffering.'

'You sure don't look it!'

'Well! Rest assured I feel it. You on the other hand are disgustingly chirpy! How do you do it?'

Deeja giggled. 'When you have two brothers believe me you have to know how to survive. I may have been born a girl but I can drink and smoke my brothers under the table.'

'Wow!' Arjuna said sarcastically, 'Such achievements! And for a nice young Muslim girl at that. Any mother would be proud to have you as a daughter-in-law. Welcome to the family dear, how would you like your whisky-soda? On the rocks?'

'Oh what a typical male Sri Lankan reaction.' Deeja rolled her eyes theatrically. 'What's good for the gander is not good for the goose eh? Are you telling me that Christine is a teetotaller? That you don't know any woman who drinks and smokes? Jesus! What century do you live in?'

'Okay, Okay! Maybe I am jealous that you are coping better than I am after our little session last night. So what's new?' Arjuna perched on the windowsill and adjusted his posture so that his legs swung loose above the floor.

'Well, other than America still bombing Iraq, when I last checked nothing new had happened in the last eight hours.' Then after a slight pause, 'Don't you miss Christine?' Deeja casually threw the question at him as she fiddled with her notepad.

'Yeah I do!' he responded a trifle defensively. 'But I have got used to it now. I know she is not there on a joy ride, she has gone to earn more money. She's been away for a year now and you get used to it, you know. We haven't been doing well here so she has gone to see if she can rustle up some investors to inject some cash! Moolah! Fuckin dough - whatever you may call it, into the place. Filthy lucre - Can't live without it...' He shrugged mockingly, jumped down from the sill and came towards Deeja. 'So you see I am a kept man or that is what the villagers call me. My wife works, and I? I lounge about, enjoying my gardens, living the good old *walauwa* life. I am a true blue Arya Sinhala man. Haven't you noticed, we send our women off to the Middle East and eat, drink and fool around with the money they virtually die to earn.'

'Don't be silly Arjuna, don't talk so flippantly about what you do. You do a lot around here.'

'You're right, I should not talk like this, so let's not get into this *muspenthu* depressing conversation.' He stopped short and smiled, forcing her to smile back at him. 'What about you?' he said abruptly changing the subject, 'don't you have any stories to tell? Didn't you have someone like Sheila Ayah who rocked you violently to sleep?' He dragged a chair out from under the table, turned it around and sat astride resting his chin on his folded arms.

She smiled. 'I had a Beeriamme who was so deaf that once when my pram fell into the drain with me in it, I had to stay there for hours bawling my head off until my parents came to investigate the cause of my distress. Poor Beeriamme had fallen asleep and didn't have a clue as to what had happened. Now, of course I was too young to remember all that, these were stories that were told to me by my father. My father loved to tell us stories. He would act them out and we would yell and scream in encouragement. After dinner the four of us would sit on the carpet and my mother would sit on the blue wing chair by the window. He would be standing, striding up and down and gesticulating furiously. When he got excited his voice would drop to a whisper which would make us get closer and strain to hear what came next. He would exaggerate of course, and my mother would sit disapprovingly on the side, shaking her head at every exaggeration and every fabrication. But we got to hear all the shenanigans our relatives had been up to. Which irresponsible uncle wanted to marry the nurse while being engaged to someone else, the aunt who ran away from boarding school, the grandfather who built a wall overnight to fox the errant tenants, the much older cousin who almost had an affair with the driver. For a long time I thought everyone's family was like mine. I thought they all had after dinner stories related to them by their father. I thought they all had perfect, funny, interesting, eccentric, lovable families like mine.'

Deeja felt a melancholia setting upon her and said to Arjuna. 'What about you? Didn't your father tell you stories?'

'My father wasn't so 'fun' if that's the word to use.'

She turned to look at Arjuna when he said that, wondering what would come next.

Arjuna continued not looking at her. 'He was a stern man. Spare the rod and spoil the child was his motto and how he used the rod. That man knew how to wield a belt so that the very sound of it slipping through the air was painful. I got belted every day. I must have been a very naughty child, don't you think?' He turned his head to look at her and found her staring at him her face contorted with an effort to control grief.

'My God Deeja! I didn't mean it. What's happened? What is the matter?'

'My father... My father...'

19

When a family has a death all other things cease to matter. Life closes down for a time. Nothing else is significant. Rasheed's death affected RaushenGul the most but his four children felt the void in different ways. Saif, the most sociable of the four reacted by going out every night after the daily kaththams, coming back in the early hours of the morning, drunk and incoherent. RaushenGul was aware of what was happening but did not have the strength to address it and hoped that it would go unnoticed by the rest of her relatives. As she heard him stumble up the stairs in the dark, she lay silently on her single bed feeling her chest constrict and release with unshed sobs of grief. She understood that being the eldest son, the responsibility of the family would pass onto him and the pressure was immense, but why oh why must he act like this.

'Oh my darling children, were you being good?' Four anxious angelic faces looked up and met RaushenGul's gaze. Lying in bed or on the floor they had been staring at books without turning the page, waiting for their mother to come home. Now that she had, they waited for the storm to break.

The phone rang. They held their breath. Listening. They waited in silence.

A fraction later, a demented RaushenGul swept into the room screaming and shouting, crazy with rage.

'Animals! Beasts! Ruffians!'

She grabbed at chairs and walking sticks in uncoordinated attempts to beat the children.

'Who did it? You *Shaitans*! Confess! *Haramis*! Who was responsible?'

They looked back at her silent. Steel in their unity.

'Khadeeja, you answer me, you are the eldest, if you do not tell me who was responsible then you will get double punishment. You were in charge of them.'

Silence.

'What is it RaushenGul?' Rasheed stood calmly in the doorway wondering what his children had done this time to drive his wife crazy.

'That was the tuition master. He says that this morning after his lesson when he looked for his bike to go home, he couldn't find it. Then he saw, neatly laid out on the drive, his bike - in pieces!'

Rasheed looked at his children in shock. Pieces! This was beyond anything he and his brothers had done when they were children. They had continually played pranks on their teachers and masters calling them names and plaguing their lives but this was cruel. The most they did was to call a master Red Lunket for wearing red underwear or recollect the time a senior student slapped a master for being liberal with his corporal punishment measures and got expelled. *Suresh Mathakada*? Remember Suresh? became a slogan of pride among students ever after whenever the Master tried to punish his students physically again.

'Saif!' he said sternly, 'did you have anything to do with this?'

'Outside!' he ordered peremptorily, while Saif hung his head and shuffled out of the room.

Later that night as Rasheed explained to his children the difference between people who had money and those who did not, Khadeeja felt great remorse, unable to bear the fact that she and her siblings had wickedly encouraged Saif to destroy the tuition master's only mode of transportation, one that he had saved for, over many years. But only RaushenGul knew that Saif was not sorry about what he had done.

⌒

RaushenGul lay stretched out on her bed while Nelum lolled at the foot.

'I feel sorry for Saif,' she began. 'He is still young, how will he cope without Rasheed to guide him? And now with this other mess, I can see that he just doesn't know whether he is coming or going.'

'He will manage,' said Nelum practically, she who had never married and didn't have children never seemed to understand the gravity of being a parent, or so thought RaushenGul.

Rasheed and she would discuss Nelum when they had their after dinner talks sitting on the bench in the back garden.

'Do you think she has ever fallen in love?'

'Yes.'

'How do you know?'

'Because I just know.'

'So, what happened?'

'It didn't work out.'

'RaushenGul!' Rasheed said in exasperation. 'You are so verbose when it comes to other things - unimportant things: house is in a mess! Car needs repair! My sister is getting on your nerves! The servants are fighting! Why can't you tell me the story of Nelum's love affair?'

RaushenGul smiled. And they said men didn't enjoy gossip!

'When Nelum was eighteen, she fell madly in love with a campus batch-mate...'

'Which university?'

'*Aandavaney*! Let me tell my story in peace, will you?'

'Ok! Ok! Go on...'

'So Nelum and that man, they were an item on campus, Peradeniya if you really want to know. Anyway, after they had run around together for about two and a half years, Nelum said that if he wanted to marry her he had to come and ask her parent's permission. So the day dawned, he came to the house, the parents received him, they were quite impressed because he had money and the correct caste, and came from a prestigious family and then it came to the horoscopes. The man said he would take the horoscopes to his excellent astrologer and off he went. But when they matched the horoscopes they found that Nelum's and this man's did not match. What to do so? While that was going on suddenly the man's family out of the blue asked if Nelum's parents were interested in getting the younger daughter married to him because they really like the family *et cetera, et cetera*. In the meantime Nelum was getting upset with the way things were going and demanded from the man if he was going to bow down to superstitious horoscopes or what? To see...' She paused dramatically while her husband gestured impatiently for her to continue. '...the man had seen Nelum's younger sister in the house, concocted the horoscope saga to avoid marrying Nelum and now wanted to marry the younger sister instead.'

RaushenGul folded her arms, allowed a Mona Lisa smile to play on her lips and waited. She looked up at the dark sky, moonless and obscure and drummed a rhythm on the edge of the bench.

'Stop teasing me men!' Rasheed scolded as he put his arm casually around her neck with affection. 'Tell me the rest of the story. What happened? What happened?'

RaushenGul laughed and continued ruefully, 'I shouldn't be laughing, it's not a laughing matter at all. Sadly for Nelum her younger sister married her man and he is now her brother-in-law.'

'What a cad!'

'Ha! Fine thing coming from you!' RaushenGul was coy.

'Me! What I did was not the same thing at all! I didn't lead anyone on saying I will marry them. My parents did all that on their own.'

'Rubbish! You also led a poor girl up the aisle, luckily your brother was there to bring her down the aisle!' RaushenGul giggled hilariously at her own joke.

'And are you sad *kunjoo* that I didn't marry Razana?' Rasheed looked tenderly at his wife who looked down as she laughed and shook her head in reply.

20

The two friends were having an after lunch chat. Nelum took care to drop in when she was sure RaushenGul's relatives would not be there. Until Rasheed's death she had never been to a Muslim funeral and while she had liked the quiet, simple and quick way the burial had taken place, she was not sure she understood this seclusion business that RaushenGul was practicing. On the one hand it seemed tranquil and calm and yet she knew that RaushenGul had issues with it.

'Now tell me how long is this waiting period for?'

'Four months and ten days.'

'Why the ten days? It seems a rather odd figure. Four months and ten days!' Nelum ruminated on the figure meditatively. 'Why not four months and fifteen days or three months and twenty three days?'

'I don't know. We don't question Nelum, we just follow.'

'Ha! As if you just follow,' Nelum mocked. 'You are the first person to always ask: Why? Wherefore? How? What? When...?'

'Ok! Ok! You can stop now. For religious matters I never ask. Anyway it's useless to ask for they themselves don't know why they ask us to do it.'

'Who are these they?'

'They! *They*! The community, the elders, the moulanas, the relatives, the whole Muslim world is They!

'But you have never been very religious RaushenGul. Why are

you listening to these *theys*? Why do you do it?'

'You don't understand Nelum. There is no choice. There is simply no choice. There is the public face of the religion and the private face. Prayer, fasting, charity they are all the private faces of my religion. No-one can force me to do any of those things, or I could lie and say that I am fasting when I am not. But this. I can't *not* stay in idda. That will be too much for them to accept.'

Nelum persisted. 'Since when do you care about the community? Come on RaushenGul what act is this you are putting on? I have never known you to do anything or say anything because someone else wanted you to do so.'

RaushenGul sighed. She knew it was a contradiction and that Nelum would never believe her but she just couldn't go against public opinion. Not now. Not at this time, when she felt so vulnerable and scared and fragile. She shook her head at Nelum, her lips pursed shut, her eyes shining with unshed tears.

'I'm sorry my dear. Forgive me for being so nasty. And it's none of my business.' Nelum enveloped RaushenGul in a tight hug. The two friends waited like that for some minutes. The call to evening prayer blew faintly into the room and as Nelum parted the white curtain that hung over the doorway and left the room, RaushenGul sank back onto the bed and stared with faraway eyes at the reddening sky that hosted a hundred swirling crows on their way home.

It had been two weeks since RaushenGul had rung up Nelum in distress.

'Where is Khadeeja?' Nelum asked cautiously.

RaushenGul shrugged. 'Dunno.'

'What do you mean dunno? Is she here? In the house? Or where…?'

'No! She left.'

'Left! Left for where?' Nelum was getting concerned.

'She has gone on a trip,' RaushenGul admitted reluctantly. 'The others don't know, so please Nelum keep this confidential. I don't know where she has gone, but she said she was going with a friend to sort out her head or something like that. It's not her head that needs to be sorted, it's this damn mess!'

'RaushenGul,' cautioned Nelum, 'I hope Khadeeja has not gone to do something foolish! I don't like this one bit! *Aiyo*! This is not good. What about the other children, do they know where she has gone?'

'If they do, they are not telling and this whole thing has come as a shock to all of them Nelum. Not just Khadeeja. They have changed so much. None of them are normal with me. Truly in a way, this idda is the best thing for me, for to be frank, I don't think I could go out and deal with the world in the state that I am in right now!' RaushenGul was close to tears and Nelum regretted bringing up the topic but she was troubled about the recent events and hoped that it would be sorted soon.

Part Three

21

'Is the liar awake?' he asked pleasantly.

'Arjuna? What is the matter with you?' she asked rubbing the afternoon drowsiness out of her eyes.

Deeja was in the gardens during the heat of the afternoon. The pretence of working had been given up some days ago but she would still take her notebooks and computer like a safety blanket with her. Sometimes she took her iPod and would lie in the hammock listening to Patrick Bruel sing *Café de Delices* or Hélène Segera wail out *Elle, tu l'aime*. She remembered Abdullah saying that her taste in music deteriorated by the second.

'This was a girl who listened to *Faith No More* and *Mettallica*! How could you do this?' he would yell out in mock horror. 'What has happened to you? What has happened to Deeja? Who are you? What have you done with her, you impostor? Give me back my Deeja, my heavy metal, techno dancing fool.'

But Deeja would stop him by putting a hand over his mouth, closing her eyes and smiling as she listened to Nitin Sawhney's *Homelands*.

Now as she felt the warm sun on her and heard the familiar songs in her ear, images of Abdullah filled her mind and she felt loved. She let the hammock rock her gently into a stupor; a patch of sunlight danced on her body and she knew in an hour she would have to move to the shade of the large tamarind tree.

It was time for her to return home. The coming away had done her good, it had put her life in perspective. This weekend, she thought dreamily, this weekend I will go home. Then she drifted off to sleep.

Arjuna strode through the gardens purposefully. His Bata slippers slapped sharply against his feet and he looked strong and fit. The years of physical labour had removed any signs of city living from him. When he came up to Deeja in the hammock he seemed surprised to see her asleep. He stopped short, his energy thrown off momentarily. Then he seated himself on a rock and watched her.

There is an old wives tale that if you stare at someone long enough while they are asleep they will wake up.

Deeja opened her eyes and wasn't sure whether she was still dreaming or whether she was awake. Arjuna was in her dream and as she caught sight of him, she smiled sleepily unsure of what was real and what was dream.

When he began to speak she became more confused.

'I said is the liar awake? But maybe I should ask why Ms Khadeeja Rasheed has such an unhealthy interest in me? He was stern, unsmiling and his body looked tense.

Deeja was on instant alert. Her notebook was in his hand and he held it like a weapon and before she could respond, Arjuna continued.

'So Miss Rasheed, what the fuck are you doing snooping around my *watte*?' He flapped the notebook aggressively at her.

Deeja swung out of the hammock, walked up to Arjuna on the rock and asked him, 'What is your problem Arjuna? What has happened? How dare you look through my things? That is *my* notebook you have in your hand!' She was outraged, shaking with fear and anger.

'My prob-e-lem Khadeeja Rasheed, as you so politely put

it, is that you were sneaking on me. Who sent you here? My bloody relatives? Those devils! Or better still was it my mother? Why can't the bitch leave me alone? So tell me, did she send you here?'

'No!' Deeja replied shortly. 'I don't even know your mother. Nobody sent me here to spy. I just needed a place to stay and happened to come across your place.'

'Tell that to the birds, woman. What a fool I was. Stupid idiot that I am, not realizing the spy you are. A bloody Colombo socialite who has come to gossip and snoop. Taking notes about me and who I am and what I do. Jesus Christ! How idiotic I was, blabbering on and on about myself to you. I don't know who you are or why you are here but you are fucking well going to tell me the truth. Bitch! I won't be surprised if your parents know my parents and they engineered to send you here. So tell me, *why* are you here? There has to be a reason, I am not buying your stupid doing research, needing a place to stay bullshit routine.' Arjuna was livid. His hands clutched the notebook shaking it for emphasis. His nostrils flared and a vein pulsed against his throat. He looked ugly and mean and yet Deeja noted that his eyes held a sliver of fear.

I suppose this is the way, Deeja thought. *I had often wondered how and now it is like this.* She had known that she would have to talk to Arjuna about why she came in the first place, but didn't know how to broach the subject. Then she thought she would just leave. Leave the estate, leave well alone, he wouldn't be the wiser and she could sort things out for herself. But now obviously, things were different, they had come to a head rather unexpectedly.

'Wait here,' she said to Arjuna, who was still seething. 'I have something to show you.' She ran towards the house and in a few minutes was back again. She gave him a packet of letters and said, 'Read them, after you have read them we will talk. Arjuna, listen to me. Maybe what I have done was wrong, but you must understand that everything I have done was done with the best of intentions.'

'The road to hell is paved with good intentions,' he snapped as he grabbed the packet from her hand.

22

Deeja managed to walk back to the house without crying. As she pulled her bag down from the top of the cupboard and put her things in it, the tears spilled down and they just wouldn't stop. *Don't cry,* she said to herself. *Don't cry, it will be all right.*

She stroked her arms as if to stroke away the feelings of agitation. She held her forehead with one hand while she threw her things into the bag with the other. She felt as if the whole world had pushed her off and she was plummeting and spinning into the darkness of space.

I am being punished, she thought, *God is punishing me for being so happy these last few weeks.*

She finished packing her bag, washed her face and looked at her puffy eyes and swollen red nose in the mirror. She went out to the side veranda to wait for Arjuna. She didn't know what he would want to do once the letters were read. He might want her out of there immediately. She had to be ready. She sat down on the wooden bench and looked out at the sun setting on the ripe paddy fields. She saw the little children go home with water pots balanced on their immature hips, she watched the trees bow with the heaviness of homing birds and she waited.

While she sat there Deeja recounted mentally the days on the estate, the conversations she and Arjuna had, the times spent in the gardens, the meals they ate. Once she asked Arjuna about Swaris.

Why he never spoke.

'Swaris can't speak,' Arjuna said simply yet waiting for Swaris to leave them before he said that.

'Why?' she asked. 'Is he *bihiri*?'

'No, he's not deaf,' Arjuna seemed to have a problem explaining Swaris's situation to her. 'Swaris can't speak,' he said very slowly, looking intensely at her, 'because his tongue has been cut off.'

'Oh my God! That's terrible.' Deeja put her fork down; she felt the food in her stomach heave over and she put her hands on her lap to stop them from shaking. She found these days she had no head for violence or violent things. 'Who would do such a terrible thing to Swaris?'

'The JVP would,' said Arjuna.

Deeja could only look helplessly at Arjuna as he recounted Swaris's story. She knew all about the JVP and even though she had been in America at that time, their terror tactics and the government's equally violent response was a time in her country's history that exposed the sheer brutality of power, the outcome of frustration, and the pure white rage of revenge.

The *Janatha Vikmuthi Peramuna*, JVP. At one time that very name would strike fear in the people's heart. What did she know of the JVP? For her they were a leftist, somewhat underground political organisation that had capitalised on the lack of basic needs of the people to inflict violence on those that suffered most. The common man and the common woman.

'The JVP had issued a hartal to stop work for a week,' Arjuna continued. 'Swaris was in charge of the much larger *watte* at that time. He went to be a big man and told the workers to disobey the hartal and if they didn't come to work they would be sacked. The people around here are poor. Jobs are few and far between and they knew that if they lost their job, JVP or no JVP it would be difficult to get another one, so they came to work. The JVP issued another warning and said the next time they will punish the *watte*. In the meantime, Swaris helped bury a JVP dissenter. That was like sending chilli up their arse. They came to warn him again. But Swaris was quite a *chandiya* and as stubborn as the JVP. His *watte* would never close down, he said rather brashly, and furthermore they couldn't dictate terms to him. That night he set off to inform the cops and pointed out those who had come to the house with the warnings. The police arrested the six men and tortured them cruelly. They were exhibited in the village as an example. Six men with broken bodies. One of them died later that night. A quiet burial in an unmarked grave leaving the family to mourn uncomprehendingly. Yet another unexplained disappearance that dotted the countryside of the South.

'The next night, the JVP bosses came to the house, they took Swaris and blindfolded him. They ordered the whole village to attend his trial. The punishment that befit an informer was to deprive him of his ability to speak. In front of the whole village, they cut off his tongue, then they stuffed it into his mouth and left him there. Swaris was in shock for months. He had to be taught how to eat, how to drink, the simple things of how to live again. We don't refer to what happened to him and eventually he took to drink. His wife left him and the other villagers are afraid to be seen with him, they think he is slightly *crack*. Of course after that, my father had to promise to look after Swaris for life and he is devoted to me. He loves Christine as well, he misses her when she is away.'

'Did you never want to leave this country Arjuna?' Deeja asked. She had pushed aside her plate and lost interest in her food. A sense of horror and disgust had washed over her.

'Why?' he asked simply. 'This is my country. Why should I leave it? Whatever happens to me here, whatever horrors, atrocities, deprivation of freedom, I do not for one second believe that I will leave my country. I hope you don't think that I am a nationalist in the worst sense of the word. I know it sounds extreme but I firmly believe there are very few reasons good enough to leave the country of your birth, if you know what I mean.'

'That is easy for you to say Arjuna. You are a Sinhalese. Your perspective would be vastly different if you were a Tamil or Muslim in Sri Lanka, or if you were an Indian in Fiji, or a Chinese in Malaysia.'

'So, what are you saying Deeja? Are you saying that *you* want to leave this country? I know you have spent some years abroad but don't you think of coming back? Don't you think of coming home? Don't you think of *this* country as your home?'

'Sometimes,' she began, 'during winter, when I am in the bus looking out on cold, dark, damp streets, grey skies above and temperatures that are so cold my lips have lost feeling and my cheeks burn, I think of Sri Lanka. I think of the burning heat and the sweat pouring down my back. I think of the sea and the sky and the hard monsoon rain turning the roads into little rivers. I think of belching buses and crowded roads with undisciplined drivers horning and then, when I think of all those things, I forget the cold, I forget the drudgery of winter, the harshness of being alone. I remember that I have a country, that I belong somewhere else.'

'You are a funny girl Deeja,' Arjuna said with a laugh. 'You think of the most *puduma* things. Other people would think of the pleasant memories of Sri Lanka, instead you think of traffic and rain and heat. I'm sure there must be some Sri Lankans who do think of those things to stay away, not to put a smile on their face.'

Deeja looked at him with a rueful smile. 'I suppose I am strange really,' she gave a small shrug. 'When I was a child I always wanted to live in a church. Not to become a nun or anything like that, just to live in a church. I thought that churches had a certain air of aloofness about them. Churches are unlike mosques or temples, they are sombre and hollow and even if they are full of people they never seem to lose their serenity.'

Arjuna looked at her with some amazement. 'That's funny,' he said, 'I always thought churches were unwelcoming places.' He paused slightly, 'I never thought of them as serene or peaceful places. It must be because I went to a Catholic school run by brothers who were so stern and inhuman. I have always said that I was never taught anything of worth in school, they did not equip me for life as we know it.' He grinned cheekily at her and continued, 'On the other hand, as long as we are on the subject of places of worship I rather like Hindu temples, they are always so full of life, there is something happening all the time. Bells ringing, poojas being performed, fires being lit. It seems a religion that reaches out to the people. Come and worship it says, it is fun.' They laughed heartily and as she returned his high five felt her arm brush against his. It tingled she remembered later with surprise.

'I doubt that religion has ever been sold to people as fun!' Deeja grinned. She was weakly amused at his attitude. 'For centuries religion was used to dominate and oppress people; more blood has been shed in the name of religion worldwide than for any other cause. So that makes me question it. Has it lost its purpose? Do we have to look at religion in new ways now?'

'Blasphemy, woman!' he said with a wicked grin. 'Especially for a Muslim woman to say these things.'

'But that again should be taken up,' she replied with a thoughtful frown, 'just because you are born into a religion, does it mean that you have to adhere to it for life?' She looked at Arjuna inquiringly but he did not reply. 'Belonging to a religion,' she continued, 'is an accident of birth. Faith cannot be imposed, it is either there or it isn't. How can a religion force you to belong to it? You cannot issue a death sentence because someone says he no longer believes.'

'So what are you saying? Do you believe in a religion?'

Her hands wandered all over before she replied. She tugged at her hair, rubbed her arms and eventually folded them across her stomach. She looked like a little philosopher seated cross-legged on the bench. 'I don't know if I can answer that question, all I do know is that I have problems with organized religion. Anyway, why all these questions Arjuna? My God! Almost sounds as if I am in the fourth floor. How about you? What do you believe in?'

Arjuna paused as he lit the cigarette he had been rolling, 'I must say that for most times I do not believe. I find it hard to believe in the good, kind, forgiving, merciful God you know. It's a bit over the top, if I can say that. I was brought up a Buddhist but that again is a philosophy and not a religion, if you know what I mean.'

'But don't you think Buddhism has become a religion?'

'Yes it has and I think that is because most humans have the need for a God.' He took a deep puff and looked up at the sky for a moment. The two of them waited for a beat of a second in silence while the word *God* scudded around her head like a puff of cloud in a clear blue sky. Then he continued and broke her spell of concentration. 'Buddhism is actually a complicated and deep philosophy. It is not for everyone. It cannot be. You need to be on a higher spiritual level to even begin to understand Buddhism, so how can you expect ordinary beings to claim they understand it just because of an accident of birth?' He spat a curl of tobacco into the grass. 'How on earth can a country be a Buddhist country? Well actually it can but it will not be able to survive as part of the global system. Most people need life to be simplistic, reward for good, punishment for evil.' Deeja stayed silent. She understood that Arjuna did not have much opportunity to share his thoughts living out here as if in solitary confinement. The words poured out of him like a flood. She looked at him with tenderness. She was beginning to understand him.

Arjuna took a few more puffs of his cigarette, he looked at Deeja thoughtfully. He continued in a voice which had become soft and mocking. 'And then you have people like me. The bizarre beings of life for I see things in a different way. You know how when there has been some natural disaster, earthquake, floods, avalanche and then they are able to rescue people who have survived those conditions for days or weeks. Everybody says at that point, it's a miracle! God saved them. But in my screwed up little mind, I think, hey! Think about it, it was God in the first place who sent them the earthquake, flood, avalanche, whatever, so why thank God for something he started? Maybe, just maybe it was God's intention to kill everybody and who knows maybe it was actually the devil who saved those people just to thwart God. After all isn't the devil always in opposition to God? So whom should they really be thanking for having saved their lives?' At that moment, as he finished speaking, Deeja thought he did look a little devilish with his slicked back hair, his mocking eyes and his wicked smile.

'Sheesh Arjuna! You really are screwed up!' She thought about it a bit more and the little smile became a big smile and soon they were rolling around laughing loudly at the thought of the devil running around saving people just to thwart God!

'Ha! Ha! Another one saved!' said Arjuna, giggling uproariously, slapping his arms vigorously.

'Thought you could kill them all didn't you, well you were wrong, wrong, wrong!' added Deeja wickedly. They were enjoying themselves hugely. Then just as suddenly as they began laughing they stopped. The conversation turned.

'Don't you have anyone in your life?' he asked.

Deeja paused, 'I do. I did. I mean there is someone but now I'm not sure what will happen.'

'Why? Have you undergone some drastic change? Has something else happened?' He leaned towards her and even though there was a slight smile that played on the corners of his mouth, his eyes were deadly serious.

'Quite a forward Peter aren't you? Anyway, he doesn't live in this country. He is not Sri Lankan and coming back has changed a lot of things for me. Do you mind,' she said, 'I'd rather not talk about it.'

'Of course,' he replied and an air of delicateness hung over them.

⌒

In the privacy of her room Deeja took her wallet out. She extracted a small passport photograph of Abdullah with difficulty. Stored in the wallet for so long the photograph was now bestowed with wrinkles and frowns. Abdullah's face stared out at her, smiling and open. She closed her eyes and held the photograph to her lips. How much had changed she thought. Oh Abdullah what am I doing? What have I done? I am another person now; how do I explain all this to you. All that I took for granted has *poof*! just vanished. What will happen now? Who knows?

⌒

Arjuna came back around midnight to the estate. He found Deeja seated upright but asleep on the bench. He stood for a long time looking at her. He came close to her and bent down examining her face, looking at her hands and her hair. Then he carried her to her bed, she murmured and called him Abdullah.

That night Arjuna slept heavily. He had bad dreams and even though he knew he was dreaming, didn't wake up. He went down at six the next morning and found Deeja already up and dressed, her cup of tea lay untouched by her on the table and she had an air of loss about her.

'Not like this,' he said looking at her.

'I know,' she replied, 'I know.'

'So why the hell did you do it like this?'

Arjuna whom she had never known look anything but strong, looked helplessly at her. He sat down heavily and ran his fingers through his hair. His sarong was creased and his shirt rumpled.

How could Deeja explain something she had no explanation for?

23

18th November 1980
Madras, India

Dear RaushenGul,

Wappa has instructed me to write to you and inform you of our return on the 10th of December. Baby Aunty has written to us and given us the news of what has happened and so we are cutting short our pilgrimage to Nagore. Wappa and I are very angry over what has been done and he says he is disappointed in you.

On other news we visited Omar and he has settled down very well in Medical School. Of course, he doesn't like the food. He will come back in January for two weeks.

With Salaams to you and the rest of the family,

Umma

12th November 1980
Colombo

Dear Sara Daatha,

I hope you and Machaan are keeping well. By the grace of God we are in good health here in Colombo. The children get their school holidays early December and we are thinking of going up to the hills with them for one week. How is Omar? Is he enjoying medical college?

We have been having rain non-stop for the past week. I hope the weather there is better. How is the food there? Please tell Machaan to be careful of the water and not eat too many mangoes.

The other day I met Harmil maini and she told me something strange about your RaushenGul. She had come for Maami's poopandal, which by the way went off very well, and she took me to a side with her eyes big as ever and her tongue almost hanging out. I knew she had something juicy to say but for one moment I never thought in my wildest dreams it will be about our dear RaushenGul. She asked me all excited if I had heard about RaushenGul and I said No! Wondering with great happiness if RaushenGul was pregnant and if as usual I was the last to know. But no! Instead, she tells me that RaushenGul has gone mad and adopted a little girl. At first I couldn't believe it. RaushenGul! Our RaushenGul, can't be, I said. RaushenGul would never do such a thing. But Sara Daatha, she insisted and she was so convinced of it, that I thought I must make a few inquiries. At the poopandal I discovered that everyone had heard about it but me. So as usual I was the last to know.

Now, I am asking you if you know anything about this nonsense and why wasn't I told. After all I am RaushenGul's aunt. Your sister! You should tell Machaan something has happened and take the next plane out of India and come back to Ceylon to look after your family.

With Salaams,

Baby

12th December 1980
Colombo

Dear Daatha,

I hope this letter finds you and your family in good health. How is everything with you in Kegalle? I hope that Riyaz Machaan and the children are in good health.

I tried giving you a trunk call but the lines are down because of the rains. So I decided to send you this letter. I didn't send a telegram because I didn't want Riyaz Machaan to get worried.

We are having a small problem here at home and I don't know what to do about it. I think it is best if you can come to Colombo and have a small talk with RaushenGul. I don't know what has come over this child but she has gone and adopted a little girl and no-one knows what to do about it. Anyway, you must be knowing all about it by now. The whole of Colombo can't seem to talk about anything else. I am asking you to do this for me because I think RaushenGul will listen to you.

With Salaams and may Allah's blessings be upon you and your family,

Sara

17th December 1980
Kegalle

Dear Sara,

I am coming on the 22nd and will be able to stay until this whole mess is sorted out. I have explained to Riyaz Machaan and he told me not to worry about anything and to come to Colombo and be with you. Don't worry about what RaushenGul has done. People sometimes get silly ideas into their heads and for no rhyme or reason they go and do stupid things. We will see if we can sort things out. And you can never stop other people from talking. People, especially the Shona community in Colombo love to gossip. Remember, last year when one of the Marrikar girls went and adopted her brother's child by their servant. The whole town was talking about it. But now, everyone has forgotten about it and they treat that child quite normally. Of course when the time for that child to get married comes up the whole story will be vomited out again. That is the nature of people, to dwell on the unpleasant. So don't worry and by the afternoon of the 22nd I will be there, Inshallah!

Love and Salaams to all,

Jamila Daatha

30th January 1981
Colombo

Dear Periya Maami,

Thank you for having come to Colombo and been with us. After you left for Kegalle last morning Baby Aunty came to visit us. She came with that horrible woman Harmil maini and they had terrible words with Umma and Wappa.

Harmil maini said that the child was really Rasheed's and that he had been sleeping with the cook's daughter who used to come and visit her. She also said that it was a terrible thing for our family to have had to adopt a child and that we will see what trouble we will get into when we want to give the child in marriage. Umma and Wappa were silent through the whole thing. I don't understand why they kept quiet. They may not have agreed with what I did but they don't have to sit and listen to that poisonous woman say all these things.

After Harmil maini left I told them that what she had said was tommy rot. This girl had a brother who was adopted by a family called the Gunasekeras. And it was utter nonsense them trying to pin the blame on Rasheed.

Sometimes I wish that I had never started this whole thing. But when I see the child, I have such love for her, she is such a beautiful happy child and she makes me happy. Then I feel better and I am glad that I have her in my life.

I hope you will come and visit us again soon.

With love and salaams,

Your niece
RaushenGul

July 8th 1981
Colombo

My dear Jamila Daatha,

It has been a long time since I wrote to you since your visit in January. How are you all keeping? Things here are not so good. I am so tired Daatha, so tired of all the trouble our family has gone through on account of RaushenGul and that child. I am slowly coming to terms with the whole thing and I understand that I must support RaushenGul. It can't be easy for her either, her Wappa doesn't speak to her anymore on account of this adoption and doesn't speak to the child either. That must break her heart as his is broken as well. He loved her so much. He actually spoilt her and see what has happened?

Then the stories Daatha, the stories that have been spread around this adoption. First they said it was Rasheed's by some other woman, then they said it was Rasheed's sister's love child by some neighbour of theirs. You know, Rasheed's unmarried sister, they said all these nasty stories about that poor woman. In the end I had to go and ask RaushenGul just how she got this child. Then she tells me that her Sinhalese friend Nelum wanted to adopt a child and so she went with Nelum to the convent. When they went there, they told Nelum that she can't adopt children as she is not married. Then RaushenGul says that just as they were walking out this little baby just put her hands up towards her and that she felt that she had to have that baby!

I know Dhaatha that RaushenGul and Rasheed had been trying to have a child for a long time but I certainly don't approve of adoption.

And what about this child's brother? It is not good to separate siblings. RaushenGul says she knows the other party who adopted the brother and that when the time comes she will talk to them about it - maybe, she says.

I don't know what madness came over RaushenGul, but this little girl she said, looked at her with big black eyes and smiled and RaushenGul told me that she felt she was destined for this child. She said she knew Rasheed wouldn't object to it. Between you and me that Rasheed is besotted with my daughter and lets her get away with too much. That is the main trouble here. First the father spoils her, now the husband!

Anyway, she tells that silly Nelum that she will take the girl and that kaffir woman also encourages her in this foolishness, just because she couldn't adopt! I know that she must have pushed RaushenGul to do this. Don't I know my RaushenGul? She doesn't have the nerve to act on her own. Then did they ask where this baby came from? Who her parents were? What kind of family did she belong to? What about her brother? No! Did she think for one minute how this will affect our family? How will we hold our heads up? No! This RaushenGul just selfishly went ahead and did what she wanted to do because she felt like it. Can you imagine that!

I am so tired Daatha. I am tired of the shouting, the fights, the sorrow that has been brought on our family. But now, we are slowly, slowly trying to make things better. I have asked RaushenGul to bring the child more often because what is done is done, we can't punish an innocent child for something she didn't do. Hopefully one day, her Wappa will learn to accept the child also.

With salaams,

Sara

10th October 1982
Galle

Dear Umma,

I hope that Wappa and you are keeping in good health. I am unable to come to Colombo as you requested because Yusuf has to travel to Jaffna this weekend and has asked me to come with him. He has been asked to conduct a medical training session at the university and we will be there for two weeks.

I read your letter very carefully and gave it much thought. I think you should be supportive of RaushenGul's decision to go ahead and legally adopt Khadeeja. The child has now lived with RaushenGul and Rasheed for two years, they treat her like their own, they consider her their own and I think the wisest move is for them to make her their own legally. Maybe you and Wappa don't approve of it, but she is not asking both of you to look after the child, she and Rasheed are doing that quite well. There is no doubt that they adore the child, in fact RaushenGul is now pregnant and she thinks it's because she has Khadeeja in the house with her. You know how long she had been trying for a child.

Umma, you are too influenced by what other people say, it doesn't matter what Baby Aunty thinks or what Harmil maini says. Harmil maini is a pathetic woman who doesn't have much of a life of her own. You, yourself have told me that she is a poisonous woman who minds other people's business and thrives on their misery and unhappiness. So why are you giving this woman the luxury of being happy at your unhap-

piness? That woman has nothing much to be happy about herself. But enough about her, our concern should be RaushenGul and Khadeeja. If you and Wappa can be generous enough in your hearts to accept Khadeeja as RaushenGul's and Rasheed's daughter I will be grateful. I plead their cause not only because RaushenGul is my sister and I love her dearly but also because Khadeeja is an innocent child. She didn't do anything wrong. She was brought into this world and if RaushenGul and Rasheed want to give her a better life, then I will support them as I hope you and Wappa would as well.

With great affection, your loving daughter,

Yasmin

15th August 1983
London

My dear RaushenGul,

I have wanted to write to you for some days now, especially when I hear of the riots that happened in Colombo. What a terrible thing to befall our country, but you know the news coming here is that it was all orchestrated, that the goons had election lists and were going from house to house seeking Tamils. I cannot believe our country has been reduced to this inhuman behaviour. We never had such things happen before no? How we all lived in peace and harmony before. It is tragic to even write about these things.

Onto happier events, London is fabulous! I cannot explain how lovely it is to be here and visit museums, go to the theatre, (6 plays, 2 musicals, in six days - not bad no?) meet up with friends. You will not believe who I bumped into at one of these dinners. Percy and Shirani Gunasekera. Ring a bell? They had the BOY with them, he was so cute! First time I was seeing him, remember he had been taken that morning only. He has two sisters there. The Gunasekera's seem quite nice, she is Lydia Akka's sister in law's niece. So now write and tell me what you want from here, the sales are fabulous! They are still on and I can get you a little something from here, not to worry.

Now I want you to look after yourself, I think the old wives' tale is true about bringing a child into the house and getting a child. See what happened? I am sure Rasheed is thrilled about the whole thing. Hoping to be back mid-September.

Till then, with love,

Nelum

17th January 1985

Dear Rashengool Aunty

We wahnt to tell you that we dont liK playine with erdoptad childrn. Tell Kadija not to play wit us anymor.

Signed
Omar
Zara
Leila
Zainab

13th November 1986

Darling Mumy and Dady

We would first like to wish you both a haipy eniversary. But first we want to tell you thet we are wery angri you didn't inwite us for yor wadding. We wached the hole thing frum heven and thort you lookd wery nice. If you had inwite us we wud hav come.

With lots and lots and
lots and lots of love

Sabrina - Saif - KhaDeeja - Tariq

4th February 1994
New York

Dear RaushenGul,

I do hope this letter finds your family in good health. Yusuf and I are settling down to life in America. It is bitterly cold at the moment and I try not to leave the house if I can. The children love the snow and seem to be enjoying school. They say it's really different here and that they can be very friendly with their teachers. How different from what it is like back home! Yusuf has to leave the house very early in the morning. He takes a packed lunch. Sandwiches which I make in the morning for him. No rice and curry lunches anymore. The children come home at 3pm and Yusuf comes around 6pm. We have an early dinner and then it's the same old routine for the next day. I have promised the children that when the weather gets better I will take them to the park and they can watch the ice-skating on the pond.

How is everyone there RaushenGul? How is Rasheed? Please tell Machaan not to work too hard and to look after his health. There has been something on my mind for a long time RaushenGul and it's about Khadeeja. Have you told Khadeeja about anything as yet? Don't you think you and Rasheed should mention something, after all she is fifteen years old now and someone else is sure to open their mouth and blab something to her. Do you want her to find out in that manner? Don't you think you and Rasheed should be the ones to tell her?

RaushenGul, I was one of the few people who supported you in your adoption of Khadeeja. I defended you and fought your case with Umma and Wappa but I also think that you should tell that child the truth. It is not good to hide these things. You should not act as if it's a shameful thing. I personally think it's a wonderful thing, to take a child who does not have parents and to give her a loving and happy home, which I know that you and Rasheed have done for Khadeeja. So I think before she hears it from someone else or before she hears it in another way, you and Rasheed should consider telling the child.

I look forward to your letters so please continue to write as regularly as you do. I never hear from Wappa but Umma does write to me every few months. I know that they didn't like Yusuf and me leaving the country with the children, but I feel this was a chance we couldn't miss.

Yusuf and I would like it very much if you, Rasheed and the children came here for a visit. His contract finishes in five years so don't wait too long to visit us.

May God keep you in his care.

With love,

Yasmin

10th August 1998
Brentwood
Los Angeles

My dear RaushenGul,

I am so delighted to hear that Khadeeja will be coming to California to attend university. The Claremont Colleges are a good academic setting. They are not as big as the other universities and she will get a good education there. It would have been much nicer if she had chosen a university closer to us, for I know that she was accepted both at UCLA and USC but still it is not too far away and we will make an effort to drive down to see her as frequently as possible. But you must also insist that she come and stay with us as many weekends as possible. It is always so rewarding to hear when children do well. I am so proud of all your children RaushenGul, they have done very well in life and you and Rasheed must credit yourselves with having done a job well.

Life here in the fast paced US of A is just the same. Yusuf and I hardly have time for each other. His change to private practice, while very lucrative, is also extremely demanding. I am so glad that I am now back in the work-force and it is very interesting working as an occupational therapist. I have to sometimes fly around the world and now that the children are grown-up and in college I am taking on more and more assignments internationally. The last week of September I am due to fly to Burundi for a three week assignment. Yusuf as usual is grumbling about having to manage the house but I know that he supports my work and is quite proud of me in his own way. Anyway, we shall be back next year so, something else to look forward to.

I can't say about the children though. They don't want to come back just yet and it's not fair for us to expect them to. Sometimes I wonder if we did the right thing, we cannot expect them to be Sri Lankans, they are now Americans as they are so fond of telling us. You know Raushen-Gul, sometimes the choices we make in life are not the choices we wish we had made. Don't get me wrong. I am glad we came to the States but when I look at my children, I see how they will not fit into Sri Lankan society again and I am not sure that I like the American society they are in. What can I do? I can't turn the hands of time back can I? Anyway, enough of that. We'll talk when we meet, about these things.

How are Saif, Sabrina and Tariq doing? I heard that Saif had done very well in his A' Levels. Please tell him that we will be sending him a card congratulating him.

I still enjoy receiving your letters, so please send them as regularly as ever.

With much love to all over there,

Yasmin

24

'I was five years old when I first heard it. I was playing with my cousin Hanan when suddenly this bunch of other cousins came into the garden. They held hands in a circle and surrounded Hanan and me and then they started skipping and singing, 'I am not a -blank-blank-blank-blank-blank-e-d' child. They sang it over and over and I didn't understand what they were saying and so Hanan and I just waited, confused, not sure of what we had to do. Then my aunt Yasmin saw what was happening and came and carried us away and gave the other children a smack on their hands. But Hanan and I still didn't know what had happened. We just didn't know what was wrong, though we knew something was wrong.

'Then, when I was around six, you know how servants are? There was this Ayah, a really wicked creature who looked after my cousin Zara; one day while I was having my tea with Beeri-amme, she made Zara come up to me and say that I was adopted. I was six! I didn't even know what adopted meant. When I asked Zara what that was, she said it was when your mummy and daddy were not your mummy and daddy. That confused me even more. So I asked Zara who had told her this and she said her Rani Ayah had. I thought adopted was a bad word so I didn't ask my parents what it meant, instead I asked my sister Sabrina who of course being younger than I was couldn't have known any more than I did. She must have told my parents later about this because they made sure Rani Ayah got sacked and it was only as I got older that things started to make sense to me, but I didn't want to accept it I suppose. So perhaps I knew about it, somewhere deep inside, but as we had never spoken about it, it never got sorted out. It became easy, you know, it became easy to pretend it wasn't true. That my mum and dad were really my mum and dad, that my brothers and sister were really my own and that my grandfather never spoke to me until he died because he was a grouch.

'As I got older I kinda forgot I suppose, I wanted to forget maybe, I wasn't treated different from the other kids, so it was easy not to know. Not to want to know I suppose...' Khadeeja trailed off, her face serious and sad. She was close to tears but kept them from spilling over. 'That's all really,' she shrugged trying to smile. 'How did *you* get to know?'

'Oh! I always knew!' Arjuna's voice was stern and strident. 'Remember I once told you I didn't have a happy childhood. Well its easy when you don't have a fairytale life, there are no secrets. A miserable servant asks why she has to look after a *Rodi* child – someone who is lower than she is. A drunk father says why should he spend his money on a child not his own. An insensitive teacher accidentally whispers the secret to another teacher who tells it to another teacher and pretty soon the whole school knows. A bitter uncle asks loudly if bastards will inherit property which is not their birthright. So I knew all right. In fact I can't remember a time when I didn't know.

'Why do you think your mother didn't tell you? It seems like you had a wonderful family life.' There was a trace of bitterness in Arjuna's voice.

'I don't know. That is something I have to go back and ask my mother, Arjuna.' Deeja sighed wearily and her shoulders dropped as if with the weight of knowledge.

'After all this you can so easily call her your mother?' he asked sardonically.

Then Deeja turned on him viciously spitting her words at him, 'You knew all along and still you referred to them as your parents. Why did you do that?'

'Not him,' Arjuna said flatly holding his palms out in front of him. 'Never him. When I knew for certain, I stopped calling him anything. I never spoke to him and tried not to look at him. But her, yes. She was my mother. Still is, actually in a weird sort of way.'

'See!' said Deeja, 'To me a biological connection is just that. Simply biological, an accident of nature. The proof is in the emotional connection. The only parents I know, are my parents.'

'Then I have no parents. Those people in Colombo are the only parents I knew but I would rather have done without them. They should have left me where I was. I would have had it better to have no illusions. No secrets. No lies. No smashed up dreams. No violence.' He stood up from his chair and at each *No* smashed his palm against the table for emphasis and each time Deeja jumped slightly at the sound and movement. She hated violence and hastened to placate him.

'Arjuna don't say those things. You don't know how it was for them? You don't know their reasons. Until then, you can't say these things.'

'Can't I?' he asked bitterly. 'I bloody well can. They took me. They chose me. I didn't choose them. I, in fact had no choice. I was like some bloody commodity. They went into a shop and I was transacted. That's the plain truth.'

A silence descended upon them. Deeja felt physically drained she didn't know what to do now.

'Arjuna,' she said, as she stood up, 'I think I should go.'

'No!' the word screamed into the trees that surrounded them. It was a word that carried pain, anger and despair. 'No! You will fucking not leave now! Who the fuck do you think you are? Walking in here as if you have some sort of right to come in and destroy all that I have created. It is my life I am talking about. A life that took so long to get on track. A life that was hated and reviled and was best forgotten. Did you not think? You bitch! Did you not think what you were going to do? Is it all about yourself? Did you not care if others got hurt in the process?'

'Stop it! You have got it all wrong. I didn't come here to ruin your life. I came here to see for myself. To see if it was true.' Deeja was wheezing. Her breath came out in ragged gasps. Her body doubled over as she felt the weight of her sorrow crush her down.

'Too bad you stupid girl! I have no sympathy for you. At least you led a charmed life. You were not living my life!'

'Did you not know?' Deeja wailed. 'Did you not know that you had a sister?'

'I knew. But I didn't know who it was.'

'And you were not interested in meeting her? In finding her?' Deeja was screaming.

'No! I couldn't care less.'

Deeja fell to the floor sobbing and howling as if her entire being was torn apart. 'If I had known earlier I would have come and looked for you, like I did now.'

'But why?' Arjuna asked coldly. 'Who are you to me? Like you said it's a purely biological thing. Just a few common fluids, and in any case they say we are brother and sister but how do we know we have the same father?' Having said that Arjuna left.

Deeja continued sobbing gently, she lay crouched on the floor a mixture of fear and anger and confusion immersed her, she felt as if nothing could ever be the same.

She didn't know how long she had lain there. The house was grey with dusk and shrouded in silence. She dusted herself off and as she washed her face saw her eyes puffy and red, making her face distorted and unrecognizable. She began to wander through the rooms in search of Arjuna or Swaris. No-one was in sight.

It was close to midnight when she decided to walk towards the gardens. Going down the gravel pathway, touching leaves and shrubs on her way as if they had some magical power to take away hurt and sorrow, Deeja stumbled her way towards the bottom of the property.

Arjuna sat in the middle of the garden. He was shirtless and his head rested on his hands covering his face. Deeja walked towards him and sat behind taking his body into her arms, holding him close. She rested her head against his curved spine, feeling his jagged breathing, his long drawn out sobs of grief. She placed her mouth against the skin of his upper body, then rested her cheek against the heat of his body.

The next day as Deeja slept uneasily in the bus back to Colombo she had a dream.

Arjuna and she were outside the house.

'Come,' she said to him, 'let's take a walk in the gardens.'

This time it was she who led and he who followed. Like that first time they entered the Garden of Taste. Deeja dressed in blue jeans, white T-shirt, rubber slippers followed by Arjuna dressed in khaki shorts, blue T-shirt and barefoot, the siblings walked in single file through the Gardens. Taste, Smell, Sound, Sight and lastly the Garden of Touch.

'The grass needs to be mowed,' she heard him say.

In ancient times grass used to represent usefulness today it has come to represent native land, replied Deeja her back to him facing outward.

Where is your native land? he asked her.

When grass is pulled out it comes to mean the surrender or conquest of a land or territory, she replied.

Can you plant it somewhere else?

When you replant it elsewhere it means that you have shifted native lands, you pledge allegiance elsewhere.

Have you planted it elsewhere? She heard him ask, putting his hands up to her face and forcing her to face him.

Deeja twisted away and looked away from him. My allegiance is elsewhere, she said and left.

25

There are times when I think that God, if such a being exists, has a fucked up sense of humour. Life is *dukka* the Buddha said. Shit! That is certainly true of mine. There are days when I wish I had not even been born.

My first memory is of London. I remember a woman whom I called Amma hugging and kissing me and two girls whom I called Vaidehi Akka and Janaki Akka. Then there was a man. A big man who would not look at me. I was four years old, a *batta* really, and I don't remember anything else about London.

Later I had other memories. Memories of pain and unhappiness, sometimes good memories but mostly bad. I remember the bed. Amma and the big man's bed. They had a *maara* high bed and you needed a *chooti* bench to help you get on to it. One day Janaki Akka and I were horsing around. We were jumping on the bed and trying to see who could jump the highest. The mattress was nice and springy, must have been new. I was sure I was winning when suddenly out of the blue the big man walked in and he was bloody annoyed about something. He flung me out of the bed and told Janaki Akka to get out of the room. He thrashed me and thrashed me and then hearing my cries Amma ran into the room screaming blue murder and took me away. I learnt a good lesson after that - never to go into that room if I could help it and if I absolutely had to, then I bloody well was not going to get on the bed. Oh! don't worry, they never told me *not* to get on the bed, they didn't have to. But even if I saw Vaidehi Akka and Janaki Akka lying down or fooling around on the bed or playing with their dolls, I vowed to myself that I would never get on the bed. I am not a tubelight, I learn my lessons fast.

It's difficult to keep calling him the big man. I was forced to call him Thaatha and even though within me I called him the big man, he gradually became my Thaatha.

It was not a very shit childhood. If you think about it you know, I suppose it wasn't even a very traumatic childhood. But hell! It was most certainly an unloved childhood.

I was still a kid when I knew I was adopted. A word here, an action there, a servant *kusukusufying* in the corner, an aunt giving me a *kunu* look, a big man, they were all ways in which I knew it. It didn't bother me too much, you know, I suppose I got used to it. I actually deluded myself that I had it better. On the days when the big man was shit to me and all, I could always tell myself that he was not my real father, you know. That my real father would never do things like this to me.

I had this little lovely dream story made up about my birth parents. Now here is a funny part - I had this secret daydream that my parents were really white people and that I had a zip secreted somewhere on my body and that when the time was right my real parents would swoop down on me, when the big man was being especially shit to me, and that they would rescue me! Then they would stand me on a box, find the zip, peel the skin off and hey presto! There I would be, a nice, clean, loved little white boy!

Now ain't that sad! Sad black Arjuna wanting to be a honky!

Jesus! I now know better anyway!

I could not be bothered to seek out my birth parents. Useless no? I was unwanted by them. Heck! maybe my real father didn't even know that I existed. I was adopted.

End of story.

What for being interested in those who had not been interested in me. Who knows the real story in these cases? My real mother must have been some young thing knocked up. It must have been difficult for her. She must have had her reasons. I don't know who or what they are. And in the end does it matter? Do I care? What ethnicity? What religion? What caste? What diseases that are congenital? What talents I have inherited? What name I was given? Do I care?

At some point of time I vaguely knew that there was a little girl who was adopted and who was my sister. How did I know that? Can't remember to tell you the truth. Could've been the big man shouting it or hearing my mother whisper it to someone over the phone.

Didn't care really. Like what difference would it have made?

Of course the idiot girl had to come and find me didn't she? Wonder how she managed to locate me? I suppose it's kinda bloody difficult to accept that she got to go to a kind loving wonderful family and that I didn't. Isn't it strange? But that's life! Tough luck! Karma I suppose.

So for me, God or whatever doesn't exist. Or if he does, then I place a shit-load of blame on his door. I would knock on his door and ask: 'Hey dude! Why me and not her? You can cut me some slack and let me have the fine life. Hey let's be generous we can both have the fine life. Why dude! Couldn't the Muslim lady have wanted a boy? These Muslim ladies they always want boys, they never want girls. So even there you dissed me?'

When I was about eight years old, we were already living in Sri Lanka and one fine day the big man stopped taking me for ice-creams. He would yell out in his big man's voice, 'Who wants ice-cream?'

And wherever we were, we would spill around him, the three of us shouting, 'Me! Me! Me!'

And he would look at us and we would be so excited, screaming and shouting and jumping around him. And then he would look at me and say in his big man voice, 'Not you Arjuna, you have not been a good boy. Vaidehi! Janaki! Come Thaatha's going to take you for an ice-cream.' The new ice-cream parlours had opened up - Gillos, Carnival, Venice, Carino's and they were like little palaces. Soft ice-creams, waffle cones, sundaes. Dim, purple lights, swirling high chairs, the coolest kids. The coolest families.

Amma would be taken also. He would force her to come even if she said she didn't want an ice-cream. She would leave the house looking at me and after a few times I just didn't bother even to cry, you know.

When I was thirteen, I ran away, or rather I tried to run away, but after packing my little school bag and going out of the house, after marching 100 yards down the road, I realized that I had nowhere to run away to. So I went to the bloody park men! How pathetic is that? There I was in Vihara Maha Devi Park clutching my school bag not knowing what else to do. Then after some time I rode the swings and slid down the matt slide and walked about and looked at all the other children there with their ayahs. Then I got *maara* hungry and had to go home. I walked into the house thinking everyone would ask me where I had disappeared to, but realized no-one had even known I had run away. Fuck! Then I knew I had become invisible.

I began to read. I read anything I could get my hands on. After I had read all the books in the house I read all the books my friends had and what their parents had and then when I had finished all of that, I started stealing books. I had no money to buy them and I didn't think I could have the luxury of being moral, you know.

One day, like usual, I went to Lake House, I made a beeline to the Literature section and studied the books that were available. The market had opened up to imported things but books were the last to be affected and the selection was miserable. Unimaginative and staid, there were the usual Shakespeare, Bronte sisters, Chaucer and other staples of classic English literature. But it was sufficient for me I suppose. That day, right at the back of the corner bookshelf I discovered *Lolita* dusty and with a crushed cover. It was such a find. I looked around the big book-store, not a bugger seemed to be even remotely interested in me. There were a few customers in the record room, another few by the textbook section and most of the employees seemed to be dozing off. As the fans whirled sleepily above and the floorboards creaked, I began to move towards the door. There is an art in these things. You have to know how to do it: you inch your way towards the exit all the time pretending to be interested in other things. You look up, you look down, anywhere but at the door. The greeting cards display, the comic book counter, the weekly news magazines that you pick up and leaf through taking your time as if you didn't have a care in the world and last because it was almost at the very entrance of the shop would be the pen display cabinet. Always Schaeffer and Parker pens on top, the cheaper Pilot pens below, mostly black with gold trimmings locked safely away. And then just when the few sleepy employees who had noticed me would be certain that I would make my way back to the cashier's counter to pay for the book I had been holding nonchalantly in my hand I made a dash for the door. Out I would hop and rush two hundred yards to the left towards the Regal Cinema. I would always time it when the ten o'clock morning show had just finished around one pm. A quick sprint and soon I would be in the throng of cinema leavers, I would join the rear of a group of young men and no-one from the Lake House bookshop would be able to even recognise what I looked like.

But today it was different. Just as I was about to make the dash, about to accelerate down the stairs and onto the pavement of the road, I felt a heavy hand on my shoulder. It was a gut wrenching grab. A grab at my shoulder that slipped down towards my shirt sleeves and held. Damn! I was caught.

While I waited in the shadowy record room that had glass windows and was air-conditioned, I began to pray. *Please God*, I said, don't let him come. *Please God*, I pleaded, *don't let him come*. As I sat there feeling vomitish and looking fixedly at the bookshop entrance while the employees in turn looked fixedly at me, and as I prayed over and over again, *Please God! Please God, don't let him come*, I saw him step into the bookshop with a heavy stamp and saw him look right through the shop, through the glass window of the record room and straight at me. I knew I was finished then.

There are times when unbidden by conscious memory, certain images flash up in your mind. You remember the way your lover looked this morning asleep and while you drive to work, you smile to yourself with fondness. You remember the office trip where you were pushed into the pool fully clothed and smoking a cigarette and through it all you continued to smoke. You remember eating mango achaaru all by yourself hidden behind the kitchen door and being found out by your sister who beat you on the head with her fists for finishing the precious treat.

And then there are the times when you remember all what the Big Man did to you when you tried to steal *Lolita* from the Lake House bookshop when you were fifteen years old. I remember it, that is enough, it is too much to ask me to relive it again in the retelling. But after that day I had no illusions left in life. I ceased to have dreams, fantasies, any of those things. I made myself live in the harsh cold reality of what was my life. It would be only a matter of three more years before I went with my mother to the depot to take the bus to Hikkaduwa.

That night, after the Big Man took me home from the bookshop, my mother totally frightened and shivering for what he had done and what he may continue to do to me took me to a friend's house. Aunty Chitra.

'Stay the night here putha,' she told me. 'I will come and get you tomorrow.'

It was late at night and all their children were already asleep. Uncle Upali was reading in the drawing room and as Aunty Chitra walked past him with me, towards the dining room, he put down his book and took off his spectacles and looked at me.

'Come here son,' he said, while Aunty Chitra gently nudged me towards him. 'Come son, you sit here with me, Aunty will bring you some dinner.' He then put his spectacles back on and took his book with one hand while with the other he held my own as I sat on the low ottoman beside him. When he finished a page, he would put the book down on his lap and turn the page, then take it up again and continue reading. He never let go of my hand, you know. After some time Aunty Chitra brought me a plate of string-hoppers, with fish curry, tomato curry, yellow mallung and green peas curry. I still remember the dinner. She stood in front of me and mixed the food with her fingers, she took a little bit of mixed up string-hoppers, added some fish, then some tomatoes, mallung and green peas and rolled them into a tight little ball which she then flicked into my open mouth. They didn't speak much to me, sometimes Uncle Upali would say something to her and she would say Huh! Or she would tell him something that had happened that morning, but her feeding and his hand holding continued uninterrupted. After dinner, they put me to bed in their spare room downstairs. They didn't talk much but after they had gone, I sat up in the bed and cried. I wept like a bloody baby because I knew it was going to be very difficult for me to live in the harsh reality of my life. I never cried again.

26

'I went to see him you know?'

RaushenGul had finished one and a half months of her idda and was in the middle of arranging her almirah. She was seated on the ground surrounded by saris, blouses, underskirts, bras, panties, soaps, powders, lotions and other various odd things.

'Whom?' she asked distractedly.

Khadeeja stood up abruptly and thought *I hate when she doesn't listen to me completely*. She sat down again and said a trifle arrogantly, 'Whom do you think? Him!'

RaushenGul put down the sari she was folding and looked at her daughter. *Where does she get this stubbornness from*, she wondered, *where does she get this haughtiness, this arrogance? Her father. He was like this. But yet she is different now, she has got harder. She has changed.*

'Him!' Khadeeja repeated and it was the way she didn't want to say a name that brought a sliver of fear into RaushenGul's throat.

'Him,' she repeated timidly, and as she began to say *oh Allah*! she saw Khadeeja nod yes. A curt nod.

RaushenGul went cold.

'When?' she asked.

'Remember I told you that I was going to clear my head?'

RaushenGul nodded. Her tongue was trapped, I am so foolish, she thought. I am so idiotic! Of course that is where she went.

Why didn't I realize that? That explains her change of mood on her return.

Khadeeja had returned a week ago just as suddenly as she left. She spoke little, looked tanned, had lost weight and acted as if she was not a part of the household. RaushenGul saw that she barely communicated with her siblings and part of her wondered if anything had been said regarding Rasheed's intestate estate.

'Does he know?' she forced herself to ask.

'Yes!'

'And...?' her mouth was getting increasingly dry. Her hands played with the saris and skirts, folding them and unfolding them in a ceaseless flurry of activity.

'And nothing. In any case it's none of your business is it?' Khadeeja said cruelly. 'He is certainly not your business and I am barely.' She got up and walked out of the room and RaushenGul who had shown restraint in grief when her husband died, began to heave and sob, folding her body over her clothes that lay around her in disarray.

27

RaushenGul looked at Shirani Gunasekera seated in front of her. Dressed in a mute pink sari, Shirani played over and over again with her sari pleats, arranging and rearranging them, occasionally looking out of the window, sometimes giving the room a quick once over but hardly ever looking at RaushenGul. Nelum was also in the room sitting on the bed. Absently Nelum thought the room needs airing, it smells stuffy.

The meeting had been arranged by Nelum who told Shirani Gunasekera that a certain RaushenGul Rasheed, newly widowed, would like to meet her regarding a private and confidential matter. Ten o'clock then, Wednesday?

After superficial pleasantries, Nelum introduced the topic and Shirani looked inquiringly at the two of them. But as soon as she realized what was happening she became first concerned and then angry.

'I just don't understand why you had to tell her?'

'Shirani, please may I call you that? I thought I explained it all to you.' RaushenGul was forcing herself to be calm and collected. 'The child has a right to know her past. My regret is that I didn't tell her when my husband was alive. And now I know this is not the ideal way to tell a child that she is adopted.' She paused for a moment. 'It is, actually, cruel!' she said in a rush and continued, 'This fact should never have been hidden. I should have got in touch with you as soon as Khadeeja came into our family and discussed the details with you at that time.'

'Did the convent tell you that we were the other family?' Shirani breathlessly whispered bending towards RaushenGul as she spoke. 'I shall sue them! This is breach of contract! How dare they? What happened to confidentiality and privacy? Shirani was furious at the turn of events. 'If I had known what I was coming here for, I never would have agreed. It was only because Nelum asked me to and I never in my wildest dreams thought it was going to be this.' She looked at Nelum angrily. 'I don't care who your daughter really is,' she said. 'It is not my problem.'

RaushenGul panicked and frustrated, tried again. 'They both have a right to know.'

'Look,' Shirani said firmly, 'Arjuna is my son and I have a right to tell him when, where, and how…'

'Do you mean to say that he doesn't know as yet?'

Shirani sighed with irritation, 'Don't be so silly and naïve Mrs Rasheed, of course he must know, he just hasn't heard it from us.'

RushenGul was appalled. This woman is quite mad she thought. 'Well don't you think it is time to have the conversation about his adoption?'

Shirani Gunasekera crossed her legs and folded her arms. She looked stern and serious and her voice became strict. 'Look Mrs Rasheed, I think this is the height of cheek! You stick to your business and I shall stick to mine. I have never told you how to deal with your daughter and I don't think you are in a position to tell me how I am to deal with my son!'

RaushenGul felt her eyes brim over with tears. 'Nelum,' she said her voice breaking, 'help me please. Help Mrs Gunasekera understand that I did what had to be done.' RaushenGul leant across the bed reaching out to Nelum who automatically took her hand. Her long, loose, recently washed hair fell in strands across her shoulders and face. She had put on some weight during the idda and her tight sari blouse created a fold of flesh at her waist.

Still holding RaushenGul's hand, Nelum stood up and stared pleadingly at Shirani Gunasekera who merely straightened the folds of her sari pleats and got up from her chair in silence. She seemed distracted and unsympathetic and stared at RaushenGul with hard black eyes. 'I'll be off then, Mrs Rasheed,' she said shortly. 'I don't think we will be meeting each other in the future. Right?'

28

Shirani Gunasekera stepped out of the house into the bright sunshine feeling angry tears run down her cheeks. She didn't know why she was so angry with RaushenGul Rasheed. It was a seething boiling bursting anger that made her hate the woman. Why did this stupid creature have to go and ruin things, she thought, as she drove out of the gate and down the Galle Road towards Galle Face Green. She parked her car and wandered over the huge green expanse towards the sea. At the esplanade she sat down, feeling the hot sun on her head and stared out at the turquoise blue water that rolled and tumbled in an unceasing wave of turmoil.

⁀

Khadeeja paused politely at the gate to allow the waiting car to move out of the driveway. As she entered the house, she heard raised voices coming from her mother's room. She recognized her mother's voice and the other she guessed sounded like Aunty Nelum. She felt an anger as she climbed the stairs. I suppose the world knows, she thought. I suppose the world always knew. They must have sniggered behind my back, looked down on me, gossiped about me. What a stupid bloody idiot I have been. During her long walk past the park, the Town Hall, her old school, the swimming club, Independence Square and the Tennis Club

– the parameters of her childhood, Kadeeja examined her situation. I haven't even mourned my father's death properly she realized. How can I? Whom do I mourn? This man whom I adored, deceived me all my life. Lie after lie after lie the closest people who were supposed to protect and love me, wove around me. Now I don't know who I am. She entered the park and sat on a bench and looked clear eyed at the beggars who lived on the grounds. They sensed her grief and had the good sense to stay away. Cocooned in their small space of habitation she watched as they did small tasks of housekeeping – hanging clothes over low tree branches, sleeping on the earth below a large shady tree, eating, squatted close to the roots of a large banyan.

She observed the lovers entwined against tree trunks. Young and excited they giggled and kissed and shared dreams and made plans for the future. Be careful, she wanted to shout at them. It could crumble. It's all an illusion. The Buddha is right. Stop! Don't make plans. It's not worth it.

Back in her room as she lay on the bed and closed her exhausted eyes, she heard a soft knock on the door.

'Who is it?' she asked wearily.

'It's me. Sabi. Can I come in?'

Since when were we so formal, thought Khadeeja that we had to ask permission to enter each other's rooms? 'Of course,' she said as she rose and walked towards the door which opened and revealed Sabrina's face peeking around it.

Khadeeja sat on the bed with her feet tucked under her, she was determined not to begin the conversation and silently indicated that Sabrina should also sit on the bed. They sat there for a few minutes. Sabrina absorbed the atmosphere of the room and then returned to contemplate her older sister's face.

'Deej,' she began hesitantly and saw Khadeeja flinch at hearing the nickname that she had offered to Arjuna when she had introduced herself to him. 'Listen, Deej. I don't know what you are going through. I *cannot* know what you are going through. I am not big on speeches, I have never been the communicative one in this family but there is something I must say and I speak for myself. I don't care biologically who you are. It doesn't matter to me. You are *my* sister. End of story. That is all I know. That is all that is important.'

Her big speech finished, Sabrina continued looking at her sister waiting, desperately wanting a sign that would show her that Khadeeja thought the same way.

'Sabi,' Khadeeja began in a soft split voice. She cleared her throat and began again. 'Sabi, thanks for that. Yes, I needed it but you know something, if two years ago, heck, lets say a year ago, six months ago, someone brought up this scenario that I am in and asked me does it make a difference between an adoptive family and a biological family, knowing the family that I come from, I would have said no! Not at all! But look at me now. Sabi, I have a brother! A blood brother who is a wonderful human being, who has had a shitty life and who deserves better. And then I look at the brother who I thought was my own and when I hear what he has been doing behind my back – yes, I am talking about Saif – how do you think I feel? And you know something, after all this time, after the long debates about nature and nurture and all that crap, right now I want to know who I am biologically. What diseases have I inherited. Who had these *balal as* eyes that I have got which Arjuna my blood brother also has. Which parent had them? Sabi, he also knows when it is about to rain. Isn't that amazing? I want to know so much. Rationally I know it shouldn't matter but emotionally it does. I want to know why they gave us up? Did they die? Why? Why? *Why*?'

Khadeeja couldn't continue speaking. She stopped abruptly, left the bed and walked towards the window and in a few minutes felt her sister's arms around her – younger, taller and stronger. 'Even if you don't want to be my sister,' Sabrina whispered fiercely, 'I *am* your sister!'

29

----- Original Message -----
From: 'Khadeeja Rasheed' <krasheed@hotmail.com>
To: 'David Metcalf' <dmetcalf@ichrs.ch>;
Sent: Sunday, September 26, 2004 1:34 PM
Subject: Request for extension of leave

Dear David,

I am afraid that I am writing to ask you for yet another extension of leave due to unexpected developments in my personal family life. The death of my father has resulted in family complications that require my presence here. Due to the sensitive nature of the circumstances I am unable to let you know particular details of the situation until my return.

I do not expect to be back before the end of this year and I will quite understand if you are not able to keep my position for me until I come back. However, that is a chance that I will have to take. If though, you do decide to grant me this extension on a no pay basis, I shall be extremely grateful to you for your understanding and consideration in this matter.

I look forward to an early reply.

With best wishes,

Khadeeja

----- Original Message -----
From: 'David Metcalf' <dmetcalf@ichrs.ch>
To: 'Khadheeja Rasheed' <krasheed@hotmail.com>;
Sent: Tuesday, September 28, 2004 8:54 PM
Subject: Re: Request for extension of leave

Dear Khadeeja,

I hope you understand that your e-mail comes as a total surprise to me. It is ICHRS policy to grant compassionate leave of three weeks to staff members. You have now been away for almost one month having already been granted one extension of a week. We have made every effort to accommodate your request taking into consideration your family, religious and cultural obligations due to the death of your father. However, I am afraid that after much deliberation, the Human Resource Director Mr Jean-Luc Vigny and myself have decided that we are unable to grant the leave that you seek. That is until the end of the year. When you do decide to return to Geneva I look forward to having a meeting with you, but I am informing you that organizational procedure forces us to replace your position with someone else as soon as we are able to.

I have enjoyed working with you greatly and it is my great regret that your personal situation does not allow you to return sooner. I, together with your colleagues at ICHRS offer our deepest sympathy to you and your family.

With warm regards,

David

'Shirani?'

'Yes?'

'It's RaushenGul. Mrs Rasheed.'

'Oh!'

'Look Shirani, I won't take up much of your time. I know that you don't want to talk to me. I am not sure I know quite why but I suppose for the moment, until it is solved, this is the way things will be. Anyway I just wanted to let you know that when Khadeeja heard about her adoption she had gone and visited Arjuna on the estate. Did you know about this?'

Shirani was silent and a chill of alarm swept over her. Before she could respond, RaushenGul continued in a flat seemingly calm voice.

'They seem to have spoken about this situation. Khadeeja won't talk to me anymore and I was wondering if…' RaushenGul began to stumble finding it increasingly difficult to continue the conversation. The complete silence at the other end of the phone was making it almost impossible for her to continue being calm and rational.

The bitter voice that came over the phone was harsh. 'Are you happy now? You bloody woman! Are you happy now that you have not only ruined your family but you are trying to ruin mine as well? Tell me what the hell am I to do? You privileged bitch! I know all about you! You have had everything, fabulous life, fabulous husband, fabulous children and then you have to spoil it not only for your self but for everybody else.' The receiver was slammed down amidst screams of rage and anger.

As RaushenGul placed the phone back on its stand she felt her legs tremble. With Rasheed's death her whole life was being turned upside down. It's not fair, she thought, I can't cope with all this. Please God why is all this happening?

Long before Rasheed died, Nelum had a theory about life 'It is karma, RaushenGul.'

'I don't believe in karma Nelum, it is fate. It is what Allah has ordained for us.'

'You call it fate, I call it karma. But fate has no reason, it can be unfair, karma is quite reasonable and rational. You do something, then it's payback time.'

Nelum realised she sounded unsympathetic and harsh. 'Not that I am saying that people deserve their hard times but… listen I don't know how to explain this to you but my priest, when he says it, he sounds quite sensible and it does make sense.'

'Ok, so what does he say?'

'Better still, come and visit him.'

RaushenGul hesitated. She had never visited a Buddhist temple or Hindu kovil in her life. Despite her liberal outlook, religions other than her own did not impinge on her existence. True, by living in a multi-religious society she knew vaguely about the Lord Buddha, and the colourful Hindu deities but the other religion she knew most about, was Catholicism. As a result of going to a Catholic school she knew about mass; had even attended it on the sly once, had heard about the Way of the Cross and knew fragments of the prayers. *Our Father who art in heaven, hallowed be thy name. Thy kingdom come, thy will be done on earth as it is in hea-e ven.*

No harm I suppose, she thought one quiet Sunday as she accompanied Nelum on a visit to the Kelaniya temple. Outside the temple were stalls of flower sellers who upon seeing the two women began to wail a chant: *Oh! Come and buy from us, will you! Oh Come! Please Come! The Gods will bless you. Oh buy! Oh Come,* which sounded like a religious litany.

'I hate this commercialism,' Nelum muttered as she chose a bunch of flowers from the quietest flower woman. They made their offerings of swollen purple buds of Nil Manel. Nelum bowing her head and holding her palms together in obeisance, RaushenGul feeling slightly out of place, holding her hands clenched and by her stomach. When Nelum stretched herself on the ground worshipping the serene image of the larger than life Buddha, RaushenGul uncomfortably looked around wondering whether Nelum was going to engage in a long and complicated session of worship.

The temple was peaceful and calm as they walked about the compound listening to the Head Priest who explained the notion of karma.

'Kamma means action,' he said. 'Put simply, our good deeds lead to happy states, our bad deeds lead to unhappy states. When we say deed we not only mean physical actions but words and thoughts as well. Indeed we believe that the mind is the source of all deeds - be they good or evil. Thus if one speaks with a wicked mind, pain will pursue him, similarly if one speaks with a pure mind, happiness will follow him.'

Later, RaushenGul asked Nelum whether she did not see the similarity between Buddhism and Christianity and Islam in that respect. Mathew says: '*Do not commit adultery but I tell you that anyone who looks at a woman lustfully has already committed adultery with her in his heart.*'

'How do you know these things, RaushenGul?' Nelum asked in amazement.

'Catholic school. Surely you remember Nelum: bunches of little dark skinned nuns with brave moustaches and hairy legs, running around in their little nun outfits, screeching the principles of Christianity at uncontrollable dark skinned heathen children.'

They giggled at the thought.

'And Islam?' Nelum queried.

'*Niyath*, which translates as intention is everything,' replied RaushenGul.

30

Shirani Gunasekera walked towards her bedroom, mumbling incoherently to herself. She lay on the bed and clutched her pillow to her breast. Curling up like a foetus, Shirani felt the weight of her sorrow bear down upon her. Crushing her down she felt unable to manage the alienation that she felt. Outside she heard the birds singing, a *bombai muttai* man rang his shrill bell incessantly as he quick stepped down the street with his canister of candy floss. The afternoon sun dipped its rays in and out of her room as she stared vacantly in front of her. She lay in bed all evening, weeping and sobbing alternately before falling into an exhausted slumber.

The next day, she woke up with the dawn. As her eyes took in the shadows of her familiar bedroom and she found her sari crumpled and crimped around her body, she remembered the past events. Without washing her face she walked to the telephone. Shirani called Arjuna. Her heart beat with anticipation as she dialled the number. There was no answer. As she stared out of the open front door listening to the ringing phone a shadow crossed the threshold.

'Arjuna Putha!' she breathed before breaking down into sobs as she clutched him to her chest.

⌒

'You know?'

She nodded tears streaming down her cheeks. They were seated at the dining table adjacent to each other. Arjuna stretched his legs out and looked at his mother. He had taken the midnight bus to get to Colombo as early as possible. He dared not tell her that it was Khadeeja who had called him last night informing him that his mother knew of their meeting.

He reached out and took her hand in his and stroked it rhythmically saying nothing until her tears had stopped.

'Tea?'

As they drank their tea, Arjuna kept looking at his mother while she avoided his eye. Many times his mouth formed the word w*hy?* only to find that it was unable to come out. I can't hurt her, he thought. She can't take it anymore. And yet he found that all Shirani wanted to do was talk. An incessant torrent of apologies and explanations burst out of her lips.

'I thought he would love you.'

'It doesn't matter Amma. Forget it.'

'No, but you must listen to me. I really thought he would grow to love you. If I knew even half of what your life would have been like with us, I should not have been so stubborn about bringing you into it. He never wanted you, you know. It was all me. I was the one who created the situation. But I wanted you. Wanted you so much.'

'Amma, please. It's over. There is no need to go into it. He is dead. I have got a new life and I don't want you to get upset over this.'

'But it is not over. There is this girl now. This Rasheed girl. What are we going to do about that?' Shirani began to weep silently once again bowing her head over her teacup allowing her tears to plop into the cup before she stood up and went into her bedroom leaving Arjuna alone at the dining table.

31

As Khadeeja looked for Arjuna among the crowds at Galle Face Green, she wondered why he had asked her to meet him here. It was seven o'clock on a Friday evening and the green was thronged with people. Groups of families and friends sat in little clumps chatting and eating *isso vadais* and *kadale* from paper cones. Ice cream vans blared Hindi film music and bright lights adorned the periphery of the green. Little children flew kites and vendors walked about with leisurely confidence shouting their wares in special sing-song voices.

Buses engorged with school children spilled their screaming cargo who immediately dashed towards the sea, wading in their school uniforms, screeching and giggling as the waves drenched them into transparent figures of brownness.

Khadeeja dressed in blue jeans and a short-sleeved black T-shirt wandered aimlessly from one end of the green to the other. She gazed at the Galle Face Hotel resplendent on the south side of the green, a beacon of extravagant grandeur. So concentrated was she on this splendid display of colonial architecture that she was startled when a strong arm encircled her waist and took her into a solid embrace.

Arjuna watched Khadeeja for about half an hour. He had seen her wend her way up and down the green while he sat on the side smoking a cigarette and examining her intently. When he had finished his cigarette and combed his fingers through his hair, when he had straightened his shirt and run his hands up and down his trousers to dry the nervous sweat, he marched purposefully towards her.

They stood there, moulded against one another. Khadeeja's body relaxed against his strong encirclement that reassured her. She leant her head against his chest and inhaled the Sunlight soap smell of his shirt. Arjuna crushed his nose against her hair, his teeth bit into her curls and slowly began to move down the side of her cheek, small kisses spilling out of his lips. When they moved apart still holding hands and looking into each other's eyes Khadeeja understood why Arjuna had chosen Galle Face. They were just two people in a sea of humanity. They walked among the crowds of people, eating pineapple chunks sprinkled with chilli and salt and drinking Necto that stained their lips pink. Holding hands they sat on the promenade, looking out towards the black sea dotted with lit ships, feeling like ruined lovers.

32

'How is Swaris?' Khadeeja asked looking towards the lighthouse that swung its beacon of light in a steady rhythm. *Light, swing, black, light, swing, black.*

As a child she had been brought here by her father together with her brothers and sister. They had walked on the breakwater and climbed to the top of the lighthouse imagining they were sailors of old out in the deep ocean looking for signs of land after months at sea. But today with the civil war the lighthouse was out of bounds and armed guards stood alert at the barricades that were at the entrance of the road.

Maybe Arjuna had come here as well, she thought. Maybe we saw each other, maybe even played with each other. A little boy and a little girl. A brother and a sister. A stranger and a stranger.

'Swaris's father worked on the estate for my mother's father. My grandfather was a strict man who would punish his workers if he was displeased. When I used to visit the estate as a little boy, Swaris told me that when he was young his mother told him that my grandfather was really a *goni billa* who would come and take him away if he was naughty. So he would hide when my grandfather visited. One day when it was time for the coconut pluck and he was on top of a tree, he slipped and fell at my grandfather's feet. He was unhurt and my grandfather thought he was a miracle boy. Ever since then, he gave orders to the rest of the staff and his family that Swaris should be treated well. He was sent to school on the estate account and was being trained as the manager. Then the JVP troubles started and Swaris got caught. In the early days when I moved to the estate he would tell me stories of that time. It was horrible, if you know what I mean. Swaris got the reputation of being a foolish hothead in those times because he resisted the JVP. Once, when I asked him why he resisted: 'Baby Hamu Mahattaya, [he wrote] I was not a rich man neither did I come from a rich family, so to me the oppression that the JVP inflicted on us - the very people they were supposed to take care of - was of the worst kind. We had nowhere to go, we had to stay here and listen to their evil indoctrinations. Sometimes we thought that these were the people who were destroying the country with their imported ideas of Marxism and Socialism. I mean what was so original about their ideas? They say they are against westernization but this very idea of Marxism and Socialism is from the west. Who are they trying to fool? We may be villagers but we are not idiots. When I stood up to them it was a form of resistance.'

'Swaris has superb stories of growing up. You won't believe the life they had to lead. He says the JVP are a bunch of hypocrites who try to pull the wool over people's eyes.'

'Does he always write down his speech? I mean since he can't talk?'

'Sometimes he writes, sometimes he tries to talk, though he will never do it when we have company because it sounds so inhuman, and I will guess at what he is trying to say. I suppose I have lived with him for so long now that I can make some pretty good guesses.' Arjuna smiled at Deeja who smiled wistfully back at him before looking out at the sea.

'How do you know so much about the JVP and that time? I mean were you ever really affected?'

'Perhaps I wasn't directly affected, you are right. But you must imagine the psyche of the country at that time. It was as if we were crippled with life. And after what happened to Swaris, yes of course the reality struck home more closely. I think it was because of Swaris that I started talking to people about it. People like Swaris and other villagers.

'We just don't know how violent our country was. I suppose we were what... ten and eleven, maybe it didn't affect most of us Colombo people that much.'

'But I remember something, I can't remember for sure but there was something about onions and dhal.'

'Adey! You are right! I do remember that one. It was when the Indian Peace Keeping Forces came here, and the JVP went berserk. You remember they were whipping up anti-Indian feeling and made us call Bombay onions, Big onions, and Mysore Dhal, orange parippu. There was a group called... let's see, they had a complicated name. *Deshapremi* something something. Can't remember the original name but when translated it meant the People's Patriotic Front or something like that. They put out a document that essentially said anybody who opposes them would be acting against the freedom of the motherland! Their support for the armed forces did an about turn and they put out a notice that they and their family members should be killed. Then in retaliation a vigilante group supportive of the armed forces called the *Deshapremi Sinhala Tharuna Peramuna* or the Patriotic Sinhala Youth Front put out posters saying *Api ekata thopi dholahak*. You understand that don't you?'

Deeja nodded as she said 'For one of ours, twelve of yours. It sounds like a time of madness doesn't it? I remember being frightened. I am not sure of what but just a feeling of constant fear. I know our parents were very frightened.'

Arjuna nodded and continued, 'Then this same group began to circulate a letter:

Dear Father/Mother/Sister,

We know that your son/brother/husband is engaged in a brutal murder under the pretence of patriotism. Your son/brother/husband, the so-called patriot, has cruelly taken the lives of mothers like you, of sisters, of innocent little children. In addition he has started killing the family members of the heroic Sinhalese soldiers who fought against the Tamil Tigers and sacrificed their lives, in order to protect the motherland.

It is not amongst us, ourselves, the Sinhalese people, that your son/brother/husband has launched the conflict in the name of patriotism? Is it then right that you, the wife/mother/sister of this person who engages in human murder of children should be free to live? Is it not justified to put you to death? From this moment, you and all your family members must be ready to die. May you attain nirvana!

Patriotic Sinhala Youth Front

'From August 1989 mayhem ruled. We didn't know what to do. We didn't know where to go. We felt we were doomed. Can't you remember that time, we couldn't even go to school properly because of all those hartals?'

Deeja nodded, 'I am ashamed to say this but we were very protected as children. I mean I knew that these things were happening but they seemed so far away from us. Our parents were more frightened than we were. But you know almost too much about it, for someone who would have been quite young when it happened. How come?'

'That area was the hotbed of the JVP. You don't live there and not know about that time. Almost everyone there was affected, either because of the JVP or because the state thought they were JVP.'

'Why do you think we were more affected by the JVP atrocities than the LTTE?'

'Perhaps,' Arjuna replied tersely, 'because we were directly affected by the one and the other for the most part was safely many miles away. Isn't that natural?'

Arjuna fell silent as he thought about the stories he had heard from Swaris and the other villagers. He tried telling Deeja some of it. The army was killing, the JVP was killing and up north the LTTE was killing. Most often in all three cases it was the innocent ordinary citizen who got screwed. Bodies burned by the roadside on rubber tyres. Decapitated heads put on stakes and left on roundabouts. Mutilated bodies floated down the river. Mass graves, dissolving of bodies in acids baths, torture by sending barbed wire up people's anus'... He shivered and flung his morbid train of thought aside.

Silence reigned as Khadeeja digested what Arjuna had just told her.

'We are supposed to have 2,500 years of history, culture and civilization. Is this it? How can we act like animals? Where do we get such hate and anger and rage?'

Arjuna had no answers to Khadeeja's questions and as they sat side by side his arm stole around her and held her close. The salt air coated their bare skins and their hair became thick with the Indian Ocean wind.

33

Khadeeja's Notebook
October 10th 2004

Who am I?

How many times do I ask that question?

I remember one day I was invited to a party. It was a rainy late winter evening and as I got out of the car and minced my way gingerly towards the restaurant door, I wondered what on earth possessed me to wear a sari. It was not a costume that I was comfortable in. It was my wedding, engagement, special, traditional, occasion garb that I had never worn outside Sri Lanka. But this time was different, I told myself as I carefully draped the six yards of fabric round my body. I wanted to show the others that I had a cultural dress, that I was not the Western influenced babe they thought I was. The blouse was too loose and the sari pleats were on the wrong side, but who would notice, I consoled myself, I can always tell them it's a cultural difference. The soirée was an Indian 25th wedding anniversary party and apart from me and a sprinkling of white folk, the rest of the 200 invitees were representatives of splendid India. The evening went off well, many badly presented speeches, an embarrassingly inept compere and a passable dinner was compensated by the warm feeling of Indianness that surrounded the guests and the general feeling of bonhomie. Then the music started and the room came alive. This was no sterilized Western music but the pulsating drums of Asia, the chords and rhythms of a culture of millenniums. As each guest danced their way to the middle of the floor with swaying hips and twirling wrists, with arms held proudly high and feet that whirled round and round, I felt bereft. This was a cultural display that I couldn't even pretend to take part in. Despite my brown skin, my kohl rimmed eyes, my glitteringly displayed bindhi and gold woven orange sari, my feet, as if tied to stone refused to pirouette into dance. My arms lay leaden beside my body and my torso sat rigid, watching the others. Somewhere towards the middle of the night, the music changed and a group of beautiful young Punjabi girls dressed in gagra cholis and shalwar kameezs danced a series of village dances that mesmerized the others with their very youth, vibrancy and sheer beauty of movement. At that instance, a pain of jealousy tore through me. I couldn't bear to look and after a few more moments couldn't even bear to stay. I stole away to the sounds of the rhythm of the girls' feet and the pulsating sounds of the hypnotic Punjabi music that had the audience clapping and cheering. As I drove home I felt miserable. Why don't we have that? I demanded from myself. We have no collective art form, no shared identity of culture. Everything in our country is borrowed, stolen, derived or plundered from others. Our food, our dress, our language, our dance, our music our art, our religion, our literature, even our people. At that moment in time I envied the people of India with all my heart. It was a flood of envy that they had many ways of belonging and we didn't even have one.

October 11th 2004

Who am I?

Who is he?

Is he my brother and yet how can that be? I have never known him as a brother. I love him unlike a sister.

This night as I sat next to him, feeling his arms around me I felt a strange and fearful passion. Where do we go from here? It is a question I cannot ask him as I fear the answer.

I want reason banished from my heart. I want to live on the edge of insanity, to experience utter and total madness.

I think about the story he told me yesterday. Swaris' story. It is chilling and I fear for my country. I am confused he seems untouched by these horrors. Almost anesthetized from brutality. Is this what happens to a country when it turns upon itself? Do we lose the ability to feel? And yet I know that a tragedy like this will remain in our country's pores, we will always have it in our souls - this tragedy and the others that we have experienced.

October 14th 2004

Without saying a word we begin to meet. Always at the same time and place. Always with a wordless embrace. We walk to the edge of the sea, sit down and like countless other umbrella lovers we learn how the other feels. We speak and give voice to our dreams and lives. We look and feast on difference and similarity.

'I want,' I tell him unashamed of my raw desire.

He smiles and combs locks of hair from my face and cups my cheeks in his hands and smiles and then just as suddenly showers my face with kisses that burn with fire.

I shiver with craving.

We watch the sunset with a mild fire. The clouds tinged soft pink scud across the horizon.

'Look,' I say, 'there is a belief that when the sun dips below the horizon it bobs up three times before disappearing for the day. We hold hands and stare intently as the fireball sinks with startling rapidity. It doesn't come up.

Darkness comes upon us rapidly. We leave each other quickly. A sudden departure of two tortured souls. There is steel within him. Soon there will be steel within me too.

October 20th 2004

He has left without a word.

I waited at the Galle Face Green. 7pm, 8pm, 9pm.

It was no longer safe to stay there. Families packed up their straw mats and picnics. School children were long gone; vendors looked anxiously at cheap wristwatches wondering if they could leave early. I knew the food stalls would close at 11pm. Till then, they were busy bustling with activity serving unhygienic food that tastes wonderful.

They looked at me pityingly, offered food gently - kothu roti, parathas, chicken parts, mutton, shrimp, devilled, fried, curried...?

I shook my head, my heart is somewhere else.

I cannot cry.

He can spot her a mile away. The very first time at Galle Face Green as she wandered about wondering if he was going to show or not, as he sat on the steps on the side hidden by vendors and hijab garbed Muslim women, he watched her. In himself he felt a small glow that grew and lit his inner being. Then, when he could bear it no more, when he could watch no more, he went up to her and enfolded her into his being and wanted to make her his. And he realized she was his as he was hers.

'What do we do?' she asked him her brows furrowed with anxiety.

'Nothing,' he replied with a smile, 'Absolutely nothing.'

With that they began their relationship of nothing.

'Who are you?' she would ask him everyday.

'No-one.'

For ten days they meet. Everyday at Galle Face Green. 7pm. Looking, touching, talking.

That was all.

Then he went back to the estate without a word. He thought it best.

Nothing was the same since.

Part Four

34

By the time Khadeeja heard about the Tsunami it was too late and Abdullah was already winging his way to Sri Lanka. It was only late at night that she heard of the killer wave that had hit the North, East and South coasts of Sri Lanka on the 26th December at 9.05am. While she watched spell bound in front of the television unable to believe or comprehend the total destruction that it had inflicted, her phone flashed a sms. *In transit in London will be there tomorrow night. All my love Abdullah.* Her next thought was of Arjuna.

⌒

Arjuna stretched lazily as he woke up on Boxing Day. He let his hand fall gently on the curled body next to him. He turned and watched her sleep. She was a girl he had seen on his repeated visits to Unawatuna in the past two months. She had become a regular in the area and he had heard recently that she worked in a village school teaching English. They had hooked up. It was convenient for both of them.

It had become routine for Arjuna to journey down to Unawatuna every weekend. Jane would travel there from her village which was five miles from the coast and soon they became a familiar sight. Arjuna was careful to keep his life private from Jane and while she knew nothing about him, he knew almost everything about her. It was a typical story of a middle class English girl, finishing her degree and wanting to come to a third world country to feel useful. Soon, she would leave and trot out her story to hard bitten Londoners who would be impressed and use it as a party piece. Arjuna knew he was being harsh towards Jane and others like her, those who came with a genuine fervour to right injustice and help the less privileged but he also knew that the way the world was set up the help came only one way - from them to us. God forbid should any citizen from the third world, however rich, want to go to their countries and teach their poor sustainable development, their addicts, alcohol rehabilitation or any such notion.

Jane was here for two years teaching English at the village school. She lived in a mud hut within the village. The only time Arjuna had visited her, he privately admired her fortitude at using the common squatting latrine and her spartan furnishings. A blue mosquito net hung over her sleeping mat, a crude side table held a box of matches and a kerosene lantern, a couple of books were beside the bed, her clothes hung from a rope strung across the hut and her bicycle leant against a small shed that housed the outside kitchen. Her meals were delivered to her by one of the school children's mother.

Arjuna was impressed with the ease with which she had learnt Sinhala and quickly noted that she was well liked among the villagers. How many Colombo girls, he wondered, would be able to do this? Would even *want* to do this? Why is it that foreigners, young white people living in rural villages, teaching English, water conservation or bio-harvesting traditions to the farmers and rural poor, wanted to spend their gap year in this country? He doubted that affluent Sri Lankan youth would want to do this. He wondered if it was in the traditional philosophy of the Western countries that taught them to feel morally obligated to help those less fortunate.

Quite recently he had asked Jane about this and ended up having an argument.

It began when a little boy became attached to Jane on one of their visits. The scrawny child could not have been more than eight years old. Wearing a pair of faded blue shorts, he shuffled next to Jane, matching her step for step whining softly, hand outstretched looking pleadingly at her. While Arjuna flung curse words in Sinhala at the boy to go away, Jane slipped biscuits and fruit to the child.

'Stop it, Jane! You are just encouraging this nuisance.'

'Don't call him a nuisance. He is just a child.'

'Yes, he is a child. A beggar child and you are continuing to teach him to be a beggar by indulging him.'

'He wouldn't beg, if he could do something else. Like if he had enough to eat, if he could afford to be in school. Do you think he chooses this life?'

'Don't come to be hoity, toity with me, Miss.' Arjuna began to lose his temper. 'What about the beggar children in your country? Do you indulge them?'

'No! You are right, I don't. But it's different. There the state is equipped to deal with children affected by poverty. They will not tolerate parents selling their children into sexual slavery just because they are poor. They will not tolerate a child not being able to go to school because the parents cannot afford it. There are mechanisms; there is a system that will take care of them, if their parents cannot.'

'Oh my! What a wonderful and blessed country you come from. Yes, you are right; we need to protect our children. But most of all we need to protect them from your countrymen! Most of the paedophiles are white people who come from your wonderful white country, to prey on our brown children. In fact, I think hordes of you people come to my country pretending to be do-gooders to salve your conscience because the sins and ills your country perpetrates on the Third World are just too much.'

Jane was upset. This man has a lot of anger, she thought. He really hates us. But why? She felt hurt and a little outraged by Arjuna's outburst and decided to leave for her village early the next morning, cutting short her trip by two days.

That night Arjuna watched Jane pace up and down the beach. The atmosphere at dinner was strained and silent. It was not that he hated her or didn't appreciate what she was doing; it was just that it was too much. It is impossible for a people to be able to have dignity and self esteem when they were unable to care for their own people. He went up to her 'Stay,' he said. 'I'm sorry; I realize that I sounded harsh. Please stay.'

'No! I want to go. I need to go. Perhaps you are sorry for sounding harsh but I know that you really meant what you said. How do you think it makes me feel? I am not angry with you, Arjuna. But what you said hurt and I think it's best for us to be separate for a while. If you think so little of us why do you want my company at all?'

'I should turn the charge around,' Arjuna said, 'It is you people who think so little of us. That is why you are all here... But stop. I don't want to get into it again. I don't want to stop being your friend. So Ok, go if you want to, but friends?' Arjuna held out his hand and as Jane took it pulled her towards him and hugged her.

Jane's initial rigid and stiff body relaxed and she allowed herself to mould her body against his. But her mind was not at ease; her eyes welled up with unshed tears as she pressed her face against his shirt.

35

After he left Colombo, Arjuna had no news of Khadeeja. He did not make any attempt to contact her neither did he hear from her. It had been two months now and Arjuna's life had slipped into its usual routine. He was unsure if his mother was aware of what had happened between them but neither of them ever mentioned the Rasheed family.

He spent his days tending to his crop, reading and taking walks. He wrote to Christine frequently and she wrote back to him weekly. But he no longer visited the gardens. Swaris would furiously mime to him that they were looking seedy and neglected but he would turn his back on Swaris and continue with his reading. Once he saw Swaris walk determinedly towards the gardens with gardening paraphernalia, looking towards him with dark surly eyes but he did nothing and then Swaris gave up badgering him.

Sometimes he would find his mind wandering towards Khadeeja and the events that took place. He wasn't sure what to do and where to go from here. It was difficult to live life as before but he knew it was not impossible. He was a strong man, both inside and out, he knew the one thing he could do very well was survive. But is life about surviving he wondered. Is that all - just to survive. Surely there must be more.

On these kinds of days he wished that Christine was with him. Soon, he thought, soon she would be back and they could have their little life together. Long ago he remembered her telling him that life never went the way you wanted it to. But even that was ok. It's ok for a life to have sadness and misery and torment, just don't dwell on it. Easy for her to say. She hadn't lived his life.

⌒

As Christmas day drew closer, Arjuna made plans with Jane to meet in Unawatuna. Their earlier disagreement had been resolved by neither of them speaking about it. They had planned to spend two nights there and then travel further South together. It was sort of a farewell trip for Jane before she left the area to take up a teaching assignment in Anuradhapura for the next six months. She had spent weeks arranging accommodation at little hideaway spots dotted along the southern coast – Dikwella, Tangalle, Bundala, Kirinda, Yala, Kataragama and then back to Unawatuna for a final night before he went back to the estate and she went off to her new assignment. Sometimes Arjuna wondered what he was doing with Jane, other times he did not want to think of it. Of course he didn't want Christine to know about this little dalliance. Good that she is leaving, he thought. Jane did not indicate that she wanted anything permanent or continuous with Arjuna either. For all he knew, this was just part of the local experience and as soon as she went to Anuradhapura she would find another local ornament to adorn herself with. But Arjuna had no problems with that, he was in fact surprised the relationship had lasted this long.

On Christmas Day, Arjuna left the estate early to journey down to Unawatuna and found Jane already there. It was a beautiful day. The sea's azure blue reflected a cloudless sky and children screeched and played by the water's edge. Surfer dudes flexed their muscles and strutted around. Under the hot afternoon sun these long-haired dark-skinned Adonis' lounged beneath small thatched huts and rested against their boogie boards. Their eyes hidden behind dark sunglasses, Arjuna thought they looked cooler than the urban bucks. He watched them scan the beach for the friendly tourist whom they then approached speaking lilting Italian or guttural German. Their queries of *What Country, Hello*, and *What's your name*? brought shy smiles of apology to their lips as Arjuna answered them in Sinhalese as he strolled about holding Jane's hand. He noticed that this season there was a change of beach boys. The usual ones he was told had moved to other turf - further south to Tangalle where a slew of upmarket hotels had sprouted.

Arjuna loved Unawatuna. He loved it like it was his home - it answered the call of his heart - that seemed to have birthed at sea. As he watched a drunk masseur stumble across the sand lurching from tourist to tourist apologetically holding a bottle of oil and a plump wedge of aloe-vera, he thought with amusement, only in this country - only in this country could a drunk hope, even dream, that he will be hired as a masseur.

He smiled wryly as an old woman abused them in Sinhalese. *They come, they look and don't buy, so get out!* As they walked back to the hotel after having purchased five neatly wrapped joints sold by a beautiful man who earnestly asked him if he wanted anything else, Arjuna stopped in the middle of the beach and kissed Jane full on the mouth. It's not you, he wanted to say, it's not you but I am wonderfully happy today.

That evening they watched an almost full moon while lying back on the deck chairs, smoking joints, and drinking a small glass of brandy while listening to the sound of the waves crashing on the shore.

'Soon,' he told Jane, 'you will be in another part of the country, as beautiful but different. You will see another Sri Lanka, you will make friends with another man and under another almost full moon you will talk and share secrets and I will be here thinking of you.'

Jane tried to protest, but it was weak. Most probably, she thought, it is true. She was only twenty one and life stretched before her. She liked Arjuna but knew he had a wife. She didn't want anything permanent, for that matter neither did he, he seemed happy with what he had told her but then again Jane didn't know Arjuna's story. He carried secrets within him. Disturbing secrets, sad secrets, that much Jane could tell but nothing more.

That night as they made love it had no urgency or heat like before; instead it was soft, gentle and slow. And as they slept, Jane felt his arm encircle her waist through the night.

The next day they woke up early and went for their customary walk on the beach.

'It is so still,' Arjuna remarked, 'there is no breath of wind. It is almost as if the day is holding its breath.' Jane laughed at his poetic description and they sat down to breakfast feeding each other chunks of ripe mango and sweet, sweet papaw.

When the sea came it was too late to run. They heard nothing as the wall of water came towards them, noiseless and black with menace. When they realized, they stood up and watched the water come in slow motion. Twirling and whirling and boding no good. As they began to move in haste and panic it was too late. The wave picked them up and carried them to their destiny.

36

Shirani Gunasekera had become strong with grief. She felt her strength take her to the telephone and dial a number she had not called before. She heard a young voice answer and asked:

'Is that Khadeeja?'

'Yes.'

'You don't know me, dear. This is Arjuna's mother, Aunty Shirani.'

There was a pause and Shirani could only hear a fragment of rapid breathing.

'Khadeeja, have you heard about the Tsunami my dear?'

'Yes Aunty, I am just watching it on TV,' Khadeeja said politely after a short pause.

Shirani had a tightness in her chest that held her up and made her say, 'Arjuna has gone to Unawatuna my dear. I just thought you should know. I haven't heard from him and I don't know what to do.'

⁀

RaushenGul stood distraught in the middle of the room screaming and shouting and asking her eldest daughter not to go.

'This is madness Deeja, this is utter madness. What can you do? It is dangerous out there. Please I beg you. I beg you don't go. Allah! Give me strength, please don't let her go! Please!'

Khadeeja stood silently looking blankly at her mother. She could hear her mother saying something, but couldn't make out what. Ever since Shirani Gunasekera had told her that Arjuna had been in Unawatuna when the Tsunami hit, she knew he was dead. She knew it like she knew that RaushenGul was not her mother. She knew it like she knew that Shirani was not Arjuna's mother. She knew it like she knew that she was his sister.

After RaushenGul had shouted, screamed, cajoled, wept, screeched and torn her hair and after Khadeeja had watched all of this silently, she clasped RaushenGul to her breast and left the house with a small knapsack on her back. *Allahdakaval!* God keep you in his care.

It was a day since the Tsunami hit and as Khadeeja bumped her way through small inland roads towards Unawatuna she remembered Arjuna. His shape and his smile. She remembered his voice and his fingers and she thought of his estate, house and gardens and many times she smiled. And the tears spilt through her smile. Her fellow passengers asked her no questions; they were a group of young people travelling to the South with aid that they had gathered at a moment's notice on hearing of the Tsunami. The journey took seven hours. Unbeknownst to Khadeeja, the van had dropped her off at Jane's village before it continued on to Hambantota. But she had a more immediate problem to face. No-one was willing to take her to Unawatuna.

'What rubbish, it's madness down there. *May mona pissuwakda?* Why do you want to go? People are leaving that area and you want to go there? What craziness is this?'

'There is a petrol shortage, most of the sheds got flooded so no-one will take you in that direction. What if they got stranded? Everyone is saying that another Tsunami is on its way.'

Eventually an old man with a corroded scooter consented to

take her to the railway line. 'From there you will have to walk. It's not far. But its tough, the road is destroyed for the water came all the way to the railway line. Even further in some parts. But that is the furthest I will go.'

Khadeeja rode pillion and the old man sped off towards the coast.

As she travelled she saw the faces of the people. As they got closer and closer to the railway track she saw the expressions change from curiosity to suffering to pain, to distress, to grief. At the tracks the old man dropped her off and puttered away leaving her to find her way to Unawatuna. As Khadeeja trudged down the path in the direction she hoped she would find the Galle Road, she was in a state of shock. Where was the greenery, the little houses, the smiling people? Instead she saw massive destruction. It was like a war had raged for many months. The churned up mud cradled twisted bicycles, it offered misshapen furniture, ceiling fans in permanent rotation. Houses no longer stood, they leaned, they wobbled, then they were no longer there.

She was disoriented and shouted out to a passer-by to show her in which direction the Galle Road lay. It is this, he indicated to Khadeeja pointing to the chaos of mud and debris that lay around her. The road was completely buried in mud. There was no indication of boundaries or beginning or end.

⌒

By afternoon Khadeeja decided to try the hospital. No-one had seen Arjuna alive. The villagers told her of him being there with a young English girl which made Khadeeja think that they were talking about someone else but after persistent questioning she determined that it was indeed Arjuna. 'Yes, yes, it was the Walauwa Mahattaya from inland. We know him well. He came here often.' She hitched a ride in a tractor to the hospital and began the ordeal of looking for Arjuna. As she trolled up and down the wards she heard fragments of miraculous survival, grief and shock.

'Try the morgue,' the Director, a middle-aged bespectacled man told her. 'If you don't see him there, he is either unharmed or buried under some rubble.'

'He could have been with a tourist - an English girl,' Khadeeja said. 'Has an English girl been brought in?'

'Well there are lots of foreigners here and some dead ones have been brought in as well,' he said. 'Why don't you talk to the ones in the ward and see if they have seen him and his English friend.'

Khadeeja went back to the ward. They had not seen Arjuna, neither did they know who he was until suddenly a young German man said he thought that she was looking for the English teacher and her friend. 'They were there,' he told her, 'in my guest house. They were on the beach I think. I didn't see them after. The guest house was swept away...'

As Khadeeja waited outside the morgue watching lorry after lorry come and tip its cargo of dead, she tried to take her mind out of the horror that was inside the morgue. *It cannot be true, she thought, this cannot be real. I am not living this, I am dreaming. This is a bad dream, it's not real.*

'Come miss,' one of the volunteers shouted, 'there are some foreigners in this lorry.'

As Khadeeja inched fearfully towards the dead bodies neatly laid out in rows, she hoped between wanting to see Arjuna and not. Covering her nose with her handkerchief she scanned the rows of dead, looking for him. She skimmed unthinkingly over naked torsos, bruised faces, swollen limbs - praying over and over again - *Please God let me find him alive. Please God let me find him alive. Let him be ok, let him be whole, let him be unharmed.* Over and over again she recited the phrases like a mantra. Like some miraculous prayer that had the power to make things all right. That had the power to heal, the power to solve. As night fell and she still stood in the hospital yard watching the lorries come, the mantra changed almost without her knowing it. *Please God let me find him. Please God let me find him. Give him back to me. Please God he is all I have.*

37

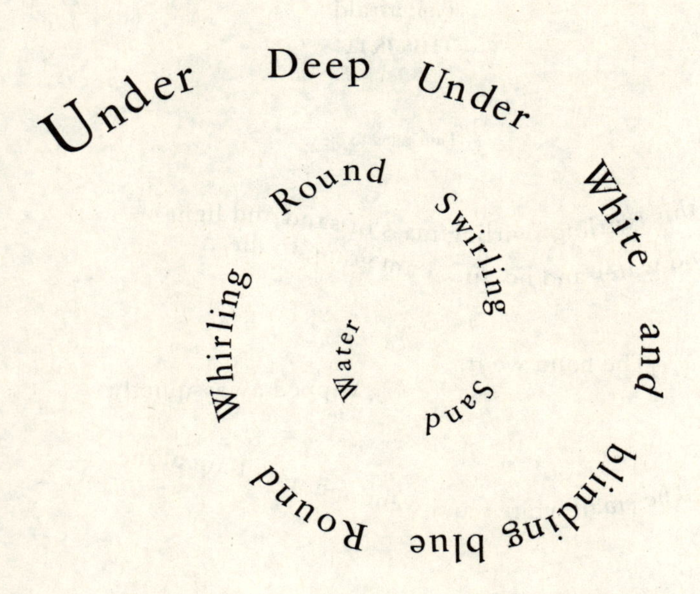

Afraid

What is this I see?

Whose hand do I hold? I Am Not

No

Not true

I *am* afraid
THIS IS IT!

I am going to die...

In this twirling swirling mass of sand and light and water and no air... I am going to die.

The hand went.

Slipped away quietly.

The small white hand went and now I am alone.

Can't breathe!

No air!

NO AIR!

Water!

Struggling.

Swallowing Water!

Darkness

Darkness now

Silence

Cottonwoolcomfort

Warm

Cocoon!

Small struggle

Afrai d?

I am ready

I think

It is now

Not afraid.

Peace

Light!

38

While Abdullah wandered through the streets of Kalmunai listening to the shocked gasps of his colleagues as they walked through the desolation of the village he replayed the conversation he had with RaushenGul the night he landed.

'Hello is that RaushenGul?'

'Yes it is. May I know who is speaking there please?'

Abdullah smiled to himself at the perfect precision of the phrase with a slight Scottish lilt.

'RaushenGul, it is Abdullah.'

'Oh! Abdullah!' He heard the relief in her voice. 'How wonderful to hear your voice. How wonderful to finally get to see you.'

'Yes! It is for me too. By the way I texted Deeja that I was coming, I hope she got the message.'

RaushenGul paused. 'She didn't mention it to me Abdullah.'

'May I speak with her then please?'

'Oh, I am sorry Abdullah, but she is not here. She left last morning. She went to the South, Abdullah and I am so worried. I didn't want her to go but she was determined, she told me she had to find Arjuna because his mother had rung her up and told her that he was...'

'...Whoa, Whoa,' Abdullah firmly said. 'Now just a minute. Hold the horses. Who are these people! Who is Arjoone and what about his mother? And how is Deeja involved?'

'I can't talk over the phone Abdullah. It's too long a story. Why don't you come over and I will explain.'

⌒

After a twelve hour journey, upon arriving in the East Coast, Abdullah prepared to assess the damage caused by the Tsunami and estimate what was needed immediately. He had read his briefing paper on the plane:

> For 20 years, the Liberation Tigers of Tamil Eelam, have waged a brutal insurgency to establish an independent state in Sri Lanka. A 2002 cease-fire stopped the fighting … but peace talks have been stalled for a year. During the fighting, 20 to 25 people died each month … The Tigers generally see Muslims, who make up about 7 percent of the population, as siding with the government. But since the waves struck on Sunday … truckloads of food and clothing have been pouring into the Muslim division from Sinhalese and Tamil areas. The people hope … the tragedy will lead the country to unify. For now, what shows is not so much unity as grief and exhaustion that have overwhelmed old divisions...

Now as he walked through the devastation nothing prepared him for what he saw. It was worse than a war. It was obliteration of entire communities. It was hundreds and thousands left homeless, destitute, and in shock. It was a disaster of Biblical proportions. Abdullah remembered a quote he had read in the Quran many years ago. *We then opened the gates of the sky pouring water, and we caused springs to gush out of the earth. The waters met to effect a predetermined decision.*

It rang through Abdullah's mind as he was shown street after street of rubble that was once the established residential quarter of the area. Over and over again he heard the stories. There were tales of horror, tragedy and miracle. Every family had lost at least one person. Some families were wiped out. Tales of babies being ripped from their mother's arms, of daughters seeing their aged parents float away battered by the debris, of women beating all odds and rescuing their children and clinging on to barbed wire just to survive were recounted endlessly. His heart constricted as mothers told him that it was as if the sea was determined to have their children and once they were taken, then the sea abated. The sea came, they said, as if it were a forty-foot serpent that towered over coconut trees. It came with silent menace, black with anger. Some fathers said how they sat in fishing boats far out at sea and could only watch the destruction that the Tsunami caused to their village and families. At the end of the day Abdullah was heartbroken.

As he lay sleepless on his bed he thought about Deeja and knew he wouldn't be able to sleep that night. He lit a cigarette and walked out onto the balcony of the guest house. He watched groups of men running about, organising the burials for the dead, unloading the goods at the mosque and talking in low whispers.

Kalmunai was a Muslim town and Abdullah was secretly glad that he was sent here for in his heart he was a closet Muslim with all the misgivings and doubts that sometimes assailed him.

39

That night as he lay on the narrow bed in the small room of the makeshift guest house, Abdullah stared out into the black sky through the small window. Why didn't Deeja tell me? he wondered. Why did she keep silent? She was all alone going through this and she didn't think fit to tell me. Why? We were going to get married. I cannot understand it. Abdullah knew that things were different now. He had been concerned when Khadeeja had stopped communicating with him but he merely put it down to pre-wedding jitters and did not want to invade her space.

How stupid of me! he thought. Here I was thinking I was giving her space and she must have thought I abandoned her. Not bothered enough about her to even pursue or insist that she talk to me about what was troubling her. I hope it's not too late now. I hope Deeja knows that I love her whoever she is, wherever she is from.

At dawn Abdullah heard the call to prayer:

Allahu Akbar, Allahu Akbar, La ila ha illallah... he took his ablutions and walked down towards the mosque.

Religion had never been important to Abdullah. He had been born a Muslim but that was all. His family practiced Islam in the spirit rather than in the ritual and by the time he entered University, Abdullah had stopped praying altogether. He didn't know what he believed in. He knew there was a God but whether it was a Muslim, Christian or any other God was of the least interest to him. But now, after seeing the devastation of the Tsunami, Abdullah needed some spiritual help and while walking towards the mosque together with a couple of hundred men all walking in the same direction he felt a sense of peace and brotherhood.

Abdullah didn't know how to pray but he fell and rose and knelt and bowed with the congregation like a wave that obeys the rules of nature. He murmured fragments of prayers from his childhood and except for the imam's utterances that swept over the worshippers and the swish of the movement of their clothes there was utter and total silence. It was one of the most beautiful moments of his life. Standing there with a community that had been crushed by the power of nature and yet radiated a sense of peace and acceptance of God's will.

We have forgotten this, thought Abdullah. In our sophistication, in our effort to live life to the fullest, we have forgotten the basics.

After prayers while giving salaams to his neighbours, Abdullah faced the first of many questions that were to become a daily routine for the next few days.

'Where are you from?'

'What is your name?'

'Muslim?'

'How old are you?'

'Are you married?'

'What are you doing here?'

⁀

As the days passed, Abdullah worked feverishly to bring some order to the devastated community. He would call RaushenGul every day but she too had not heard from Khadeeja and was worried about her.

'I have asked some cousins to go down South and look for her. They are leaving early tomorrow morning,' she told Abdullah. 'If I hear of anything I will let you know.'

40

Abdullah turned to concentrate on his work. More than thirty six hours after the Tsunami hit, the government was unable to activate an adequate relief plan. And by the time he arrived, Abdullah realized that most of the aid coming in the form of food, medical supplies and equipment were donated by individuals and local groups. The response had been overwhelming but there was only so much the citizens could do. The hospitals, the few that were still standing were overwhelmed and dead bodies stacked in neat rows were beginning to putrefy. The stench was unbearable. The mosque decided to bury the bodies.

Abdullah watched as a group of men who had appointed themselves as the burial team and who had travelled all night from Puttalam situated right across the country on the West coast, began to dig the trenches. With white bands around their heads and white handkerchiefs across their faces they looked like spiritual Jihad fighters about to go into battle. *Where are you Khadeeja my love? Is it the same where you are? How are you? Are you alone? Do you think of me? Life is so short. I am so stupid for letting you go. Don't go my love. Just don't go.*

There were eight trenches dug. About twenty feet in length and six feet deep, the trenches took all day to prepare. In the night they buried the dead. With murmured prayers and candles and incense dotting the sand, the men loaded the mass graves with bodies. It was not a time to ask about religion or ethnicity. They died together so they will be buried together, the Imam told Abdullah. It is important that they are at peace now. All souls with Allah.

The next morning he made out a list of supplies with the mosque authorities. Abdullah began to write while they listed their needs.

Medicine – Panadol (adult and children)
Bandage, cotton wool
Kitchen utensils and cups
Water
Mosquito coils
Candles
Bed sheets
Infant milk
Clothes for kids
Underwear for women
Mats, Pillows
Tents

Occasionally amidst his work his mind wandered: *Khadeeja why don't you call me? What is happening with you? Why are you silent? Have you found him? Do you not need me anymore?*

Then they gave him their lists of the displaced.

Kannakipuram..376 families
Chenaikuiruppu Ganesha Vidyalayam.......................2000 families
4th colony school..3000 families
Annamalei...3000 families
Kalmunai Patima College...5000 families
Natpatimunai Sivashakthi school.............................3000 families

The list went on and on…

Oh my love, are you going through the same thing? Call me? Please! Call your mother if you don't want to talk to me? We haven't heard anything from you for days. I'm worried. I want you to find your brother. I love you so much. Oh Khadeeja, what has happened to us?

At the office Abdullah had his first meeting. 'First,' he said, 'we must open rehabilitation centers for children.'

'What about the temporary shelters and health facilities?' Siva his assistant queried worriedly.

'That is already done, Siva. Concentrate on what *needs* to be done. We have been told that other international organizations are already in the area and they must have seen to the basics.'

'Don't be too sure about that Mr. Abdullah. I have heard reports that further up the East Coast the UN agencies are not to be seen. So let's go in expecting nothing to be there.'

'Ok, let me check on that after this briefing. But let me continue with this now. Our priority right now is the women and children. We have to look out for children who tend to be neglected by their families who they themselves are in a trauma state. We need to create a safe place for children so that the women can concentrate on the rehabilitation without the burden of children. Siva will you take Kumudini and see to that?'

'Ok Mr. Abdullah.'

Khadeeja, listen. Please. Just give a quick call my love. We can talk later. Just let me know that you are Ok. Don't do this to me. To us. I don't understand what is happening. Please. Just call me. Talk to me. Please.

'Mr. Abdullah. Mr Abdullah,' an agitated hand waved in front of Abdullah's face.

'Yes Kumudini?' Abdullah recovered his attention quickly.

'I think that the center should have lots of toys and if we could have some money for paint to put in some cheerful colours, I think that would help as well.'

'Excellent idea Kumudini,' Abdullah, embarrassed at his distraction was pleased with the quiet intelligent young woman who had joined the team at the last minute. 'Don't forget to give some special attention to girl children. They are in danger of being forgotten as they may not be as vocal as boys or act aggressively to get attention.

'Yes sir. In my previous job we were told that sometimes we think girl children are without problems because they are silent but they suffer a lot from depression.'

'That's right Kumudini. Also look into setting up a few counseling groups for the women. I think they may be more effective than the standard 'one to one' trauma therapy that the guidebooks talk about. We should focus on 'domestic violence' as well as it is a known fact that during times like these, domestic violence reaches unprecedented levels in a very short time.'

'What do you mean Mr. Abdullah?' Siva inquired with a puzzled look on his face.

'Well, when we were working in Turkey, we found out that a month after the earthquake around 80% of the women were facing domestic violence. There were many reasons for it. Men tend to be more aggressive as a result of the trauma; shrinking living space, unemployment, drinking etc. being among the major contributors. We must not forget also that sexual abuse of children can become a huge problem. Resources are scarce. We must make sure that efforts and materials do not get wasted due to lack of co-ordination. Sundari and Krishna, will you both take over the co-ordination center. Contact all the NGO's in the area. Introduce yourselves and explain the project. Get back to me at the end of the day with the preliminary information.'

'Ok sir,' they chorused as they left Abdullah who continued

sitting in the room looking out of the window, his mind already elsewhere.

Khadeeja where are you? Why have you gone away? What has happened? What about us? God! what is happening? Look after her please. Keep her in your care.

41

In the evenings Abdullah would walk around the village, speaking a few words here and there to the people. He began visiting the mosque every night after *Isha* prayers and had informal chats with the Imam over a simple dinner of *roti* and dhal.

One day he asked, 'Imam Shahul Hameed how do you explain all this? What is the meaning of this tragedy? Most of them were poor people. They had suffered immensely during the war and now this? How do you explain it? Where is the just God that we are taught?'

Imam Shahul Hameed looked quietly at this man whom he was just getting to know. He took Abdullah's soft hands within his callused and rough palms and began.

'My son,' he said, 'the whole of mankind struggles in pain and suffering. Why do people get cancer? Why are children orphaned? While we don't know the answers for this we do know that God is a God of mercy. He means for his creation to work towards healing hearts. There is a spark in mankind that comes out of tragedy. Every person has a spark of God in them. In times like these, that spark becomes a passionate flame that warms the community. Look at this place. We have people from all over the country, from all over the world. Look at you. You came to us. You and others like you have cared for us, comforted us, wept with us. In the midst of this great tragedy God gave us the most wonderful thing - he gave us hope.' The Imam paused as he fumbled for a handkerchief to wipe his brow. The little mosque built away from the sea was hot and stuffy, the lone fan circulated sluggishly ahead and the dim lights flickered and brightened with frequent power surges. After a sip of cool water from an earthenware pot beside him, the Imam continued.

'There was a philosopher who once asked why is it that when a rotten apple is put into a barrel of good apples, the good apples will become rotten but a good apple put into a barrel of rotten apples does not have the ability to make them good. In other words why did God make a world where sickness and rottenness are almost contagious? But one day I realized that even the so called good apple is not really good. It is eternally flawed. Because it has a mortal wound - where it was separated from its source of life - its stem. This is when I realized that nothing - be it fruit, vegetable or man when separated from its source of life is sound. That all are ill and only God is health and wholeness and holiness. But we have forgotten about God. And to the philosopher who was asking about why good apples cannot make rotten apples good. They can - if they are a Buddha or a Jesus or a Muhammad they can. Indeed they can.'

Abdullah felt the tears prick his eyes. He was moved and he didn't quite know why. It had been a hard few weeks and he was worried about Khadeeja. Not so much for her safety as for her mental well being.

'Tomorrow then, Imam,' he said standing up and shaking the pins and needles out of his feet.

'You are troubled my son. Do you want to stay and talk?'

Abdullah shook his head as he slipped into his sandals and putting his hand to his chest in a gesture of farewell, took his leave of the Imam.

'May God be with you son,' said the Imam as he turned around and began to pray.

42

Imam Shahul Hameed was not a learned man. Not in the worldly sense. His father was an Imam and before that his father. They had lived all their life in the town of Kalpitiya on the west coast of the island and came from an old, well respected but poor family.

When Shahul Hameed was fourteen years old a group of religious teachers came to the village. They were dressed in long white robes and wore white turbans wrapped around their heads and had piercing light brown eyes. These tall strong looking handsome men said they were looking for young intelligent boys for admission to a religious school located in the hills of Pakistan, on the outskirts of Islamabad. There they would be taught all aspects of the religion of Islam, from recitation, interpretation, jurisprudence, customs and traditions to other such important matters. Shahul Hameed, never having left the area begged his father to let him be interviewed by the men, despite the senior Hameed's reservations.

'Please Wappa; I will never get another chance like this. Think about it, it's a chance for me to get a proper education. I can be a good Imam when I return. Not that you are not a good Imam,' he added hastily not wanting to offend his father. 'But the Holy Prophet said, "Go even to China in search of knowledge."'

Shahul Hameed's father scratched his fine head of hair and rolled his tongue against his betel stained teeth and wondered about the proposition. He was a simple man who became Imam only because his father had been one before him. He was well respected in the town and many of the people came to him for advice and guidance. He knew however, that his son was intelligent and inquiring and was destined for things greater than Kalpitiya. It is true; he thought to himself, the world is changing at a great pace. If Shahul Hameed remained in the town he would be no greater than me, or his grandfather, but if he left... if he was taken by these men across the waters to other countries and was taught Islam in all its glory and complexity, why then, he could become a great Imam; he could leave Kalpitiya and join any one of the mosques in the bigger towns - Kandy, Galle, even Colombo.

And so Shahul Hameed was sent to a madrasah in Pakistan. In a matter of weeks he realized that it was going to be a painful and sorrowful mistake. Here among three hundred other young boys like himself, far from home and family brought from countries like Sri Lanka, India, South Africa, Sudan, Malaysia and Bangladesh he found himself in a religious prison. Every waking moment was devoted to the business of learning a religion that did not tolerate any deviations from the straight and narrow path determined by the authorities. The madrasah was funded by the *Wahhabi's* from Saudi Arabia who were infiltrating countries with large Muslim populations, indoctrinating them in the stern and rigid interpretation of Abdul Wahhab the charismatic religious leader who supported Ibn Saud in his quest to rule Arabia.

Rocking back and forth reciting the Holy Quran, Shahul Hameed realized that he was not going to last in the madrasah. He disagreed with the whole system that prevailed there - the unquestioning rote, the rigid hierarchy, the intolerance. This cannot be Islam he would retort and each time he queried the system he would be beaten. Sometimes he would be locked up in his room which was no bigger than a cell and given only two chapattis to eat and a glass of water to drink for the whole day. The cell had a grill on the side that looked down into the inner courtyard where he could see his friends walk to and fro between classes and where they would gather in little huddled groups whispering among themselves. Sometimes they would look up at him and wave or mouth encouragement. Then he was befriended by a young South African boy who had come like him on a scholarship.

'Shahul,' he would whisper beneath the door. 'They are coming tonight to make you apologize. Say you are sorry or else you will be beaten.'

'Even if I say I am sorry they will beat me,' Shahul Hameed would retort stubbornly. He knew that it made no difference what he did or said, the institute was run by a bunch of sadists who took out their frustrations on the students.

Eventually he ran away and when he was picked up by the police after two weeks of hide and seek he was arrested and imprisoned. After a short time in a Pakistani prison where he was sodomised every day and tortured in a hundred different ways that he did not care to remember, he found himself on a cargo boat to Colombo.

He had left when he was fourteen and the boy who returned at eighteen was a changed man. After a short apprenticeship at the mosque in Kalmunai, he succeeded the old Imam on his death and was immensely popular with the community.

The people soon realized that the new Imam used his education to seek out new and compassionate interpretations of the religion. Not content to be a passive component of the town, he gained a reputation for discussion and was fond of encouraging the youth to debate and probe intricate principles.

Imam Shahul Hameed was an unusual man in his outlook. He

took pride in being a Sri Lankan as well as being a Muslim and took pains to teach his community that the duties of a good citizen were as important as being a good devotee. In recent times he would comment on the young men who flooded the streets of Kalmunai at night wearing long robes and sporting twisted turbans on their heads. 'What is this garb?' he would laugh gently as they streamed outside his little mosque. 'It is not our dress. It is the dress of the Arabs. We are not Arabs. So why do we want to dress like Arabs? We must not lose the sense of who we are. We belong to this country that has a proud and rich history. We must not forget our contribution to this country of ours. We have no need to look elsewhere for our heritage.'

'Look Imam,' a few of them would retort lightly, 'this country seems to have no need for us, and we, we are descended from Arab traders do not forget that. So even this dress is part of our heritage.'

'Come, my son,' the Imam would reply with a smile on his lips but his eyes were serious. 'Let us examine that. Do you think the Arab traders came with their wives? No, they did not. They came here and married the women of this land. Our land. So what does that make you, more Arab or more Lankan? Before you answer the question think of where you are? In Arabia or Sri Lanka?'

'Sri Lanka,' the puzzled youth would reply.

'Then, you have your answer of who you are don't you?' the Imam said. 'If this country was good enough for your Arab forefathers, then shouldn't it be good enough for you my son?'

But the Imam knew he was fighting a hard and losing battle. Hundreds of villagers had returned from the Middle East bringing with them the strict *Wahhabi* interpretation of Islam that in his opinion broke its spirit.

He knew that they disapproved of him and his beliefs and that it may be a matter of time before an Imam more suited to their *purist* beliefs would be brought into the mosque and then, he knew he would have to leave. But in the meantime, for now, he would try to infiltrate these angry youth with his pacifist and tolerant message. That night as he went into his mosque to pray his *Isha* he felt slightly lost. 'Ya Allah! come to me tonight. I need you,' he whispered urgently.

⌒

He was fond of this young African man who came with the Tsunami aid workers. Abdullah was different from any of the foreigners he had come across and was the first African he had met. No, that is not true, the Imam, corrected himself. He remembered his young South African friend in the Madrasah. He wondered what had happened to him now. Was he broken by the madrasah, or did he survive?

43

Khadeeja was exhausted. She had not slept, she had not eaten and as she sat on the ground leaning against a pillar, dirt smeared and unwashed for the past twenty four hours, she felt a weariness descend upon her. She gazed unseeingly before her, not caring if passers-by thought she was mad. The last truck load of bodies had come and gone and Arjuna was not in any of them.

Maybe he is safe, she thought. If he is not here, he is not dead.

As the waning moon rose giving the parking lot of the morgue an appropriate air of morbidity, Khadeeja saw a young woman walk towards her, wearing jeans and a yellow T-shirt, she held out a glass of water and carried a five litre container of bottled water in her other hand.

'It's boiled and filtered water. It's safe to drink,' said the woman handing the glass to Khadeeja and sinking to the ground beside her.

Khadeeja gratefully took the glass and realized she had not eaten for over twenty four hours.

'More?' questioned the girl and then, 'Who are you looking for?'

'A friend... No sorry... not a friend... er… my brother.'

The girl continued looking at Khadeeja for a while saying nothing. Khadeeja turned her head, 'Who are you?' she asked.

'I am a volunteer. I came last morning, we are trying to recover bodies and reunite families. Describe whom you lost and I will go back and give the information to my team. There are sixty of us here. Don't worry we will find him, this brother of yours.'

Khadeeja bent her head and felt a wave of hopelessness wash over her.

'My name is Khadeeja. Khadeeja Rasheed. My brother was here in Unawatuna on Poya day. People seem to have seen him. He was with an English teacher before the wave came but no-one has seen them since. He is twenty six years old, is of average height and has longish hair.'

'I am Shani,' said the girl, 'if you have no place to stay, you can stay with us. We have rented a little guest house a mile inland where a few of us are staying.'

Khadeeja nodded gratefully and allowed the girl to lead her away towards a jeep parked at the entrance to the morgue.

The guest house was a simple one story cement house that had no electricity. There was one big room which ten of them slept in. Khadeeja sank down onto one of the reed mats and fell asleep immediately.

Shani continued looking at her and after a while went outside and lit a cigarette.

'Who's the chick?' asked one of her team mates.

Shani shrugged, 'Some woman who is looking for her brother. Maybe we can help her find him.'

'Are you mad Shani?' asked the man aggressively. 'We leave tomorrow early morning. We can't do anything for her. Maybe she can continue to stay here if she has no other place. But we did what we had to do. We came to clean up and help. Now we all have to go back as scheduled. Or else we will have no jobs to go back to.'

'This is stupid. What kind of help is this? It is white wash for our conscience. We dash down like scalded cats, help a bit and then go back to our nice quiet existence and talk about how we did relief work for the rest of our lives.'

'Well as team leader I am telling you that we leave tomorrow. If you want to stay, go ahead. Be the holier than thou creature you always make out to be. For us it's more than enough that we came and did our bit and now we have to get on with our lives. We cannot be expected to save the world on our own. Come on, girl, don't take this relief thing too much to heart. Anyway, you make up your mind, if you are coming with us, we leave in the morning. Five a.m.'

Shani saw the body first. It had been four days and he was lying on the beach face down. He had no shirt and only tatters for trousers. Could it be, she wondered? Could it be the brother? She quickly looked up to see where Khadeeja was and saw her further up the beach talking to the villagers. In her quick assessment Shani saw that the dogs had got to the torso but his face was untouched. She put her handkerchief to her nose and looked away quickly. The stench was unbearable. Her first instinct was to protect Khadeeja from discovering him but then again knew that was going to be impossible.

She stood by the body looking at Khadeeja and soon, as she knew it would happen, Khadeeja looked at her, saw something lying on the beach and began to walk towards Shani, then broke into a run. As she approached, Shani saw the tears streaming down her face. She stood by helplessly watching Khadeeja sink into the sand and turn the rotting corpse over. Watched her tears become sobs as she saw Arjuna's face and then cry as if her heart was being wrenched from her body as she absorbed the state of his battered body.

⌒

Arjuna's funeral was quiet and simple. There must have been no more than forty people who had come to the estate. Swaris had decided that he must be cremated in one of the gardens. Khadeeja did not attend. There can be no greater grief than losing a child thought Shirani as she lit the pyre. Whatever anyone says he is my child. Not of my womb but still my child. Not of my blood but still my child. Not of my ancestry but still my child. As the priest intoned - '*Where eternal luster glows, the realm in which the light divine is set, place me, Purifier, in that deathless, imperishable world. Make me immortal in that realm where movement is accordant to wish, in the third region, the third heaven of heavens, where the worlds are resplendent.*'

Shirani thought of the piece of paper she had found by Arjuna's bedside. It was handwritten in pencil and was from the Bhagavat Gita when the Pandyan Arjuna sings a hymn of praise to Lord Krishna:

Ah, my God, I see all gods within your body;
Each in his degree, the multitude of creatures;
See Lord Brahma enthroned upon his lotus;
See all the sages, and the holy serpents.

Universal Form, I see you without limit,
Infinite of arms, eyes, mouths, and bellies
See, and find no end, midst, or beginning.

Crowned with diadems, you wield the mace and discus,
Shining every way the eyes shrink from your splendor
Brilliant like the sun; like fire, blazing, boundless.

You are all we know, supreme, beyond man's measure,
This world's sure-set plinth and refuge never shaken,
Guardian of eternal law, life's Soul undying.

Birthless, deathless; yours the strength titanic,
Million-armed, the sun and moon your eyeballs,
Fiery-faced, you blast the world to ashes.

45

Abdullah was studying the form with his assistant Siva. It was ten o'clock in the morning and they puzzled over the document that had been sent through the International Disaster Rehabilitation Organisation earlier that day.

'What does this mean Mr. Abdullah?' Siva asked, as he read: 'You must have proof of ownership (your deed, tax records, mortgage payment book, or a copy of your dwelling's insurance policy for the address, showing you as owner). Are they mad?' he asked looking up at Abdullah in amazement. 'These people have nothing. They never had anything in any case, even before the Tsunami hit. If they have to depend on furnishing these documents to get aid, they will never get it.'

Abdullah sighed with frustration; he had realized when he perused the document that it had not been drafted by any intelligent person who was familiar with Asia. The project itself was laudable, its purpose to provide money and services to people in the disaster areas. The help was to include temporary housing, repair of houses, replacement of houses provided they were not located in the 100 meter no-build zone and other sundry needs for medical, funeral, transportation, moving and storage - a few essentials that would crop up. However, the rules and regulations that covered the project were more suited to the West than Asia.

'I know, Siva,' he said, 'We will have to write a report to headquarters and tell them it will be impossible to run the project the way they envision it. I am going for a joint organisation meeting this afternoon. We all have the same problems, so after consulting with Save the Children, UNHCR and Oxfam, we will draft a reply to this. Don't worry; things will work out in the end.' He patted his colleague absent-mindedly on the arm and left the room preoccupied.

Outside, he bumped into Kumudini. 'Sir, there is an urgent call for you. Come quickly a madam is crying.'

Abdullah's first thought was that something had happened to Khadeeja. Running down the corridor to the main office room, he began to feel panic rise within him.

'Hello?'

'Abdullah, this is RaushenGul,' said a teary voice.

'Yes Raushen, what is it? Have you found Khadeeja?'

There was a slight hesitation then, 'Yes.' Again another pause, then Abdullah heard RaushenGul take a deep breath and say, 'Arjuna is dead. Khadeeja found his body and the funeral is today.'

'Where is Khadeeja? Has she gone for the funeral?'

'No. She stayed behind in Unawatuna. She called me the day she found Arjuna. She arranged for his body to be dispatched back to the estate after she had spoken to his mother and then she said she wanted to stay in the area for a few more days. She has joined some relief team I think. She said she will call me in a few days again.'

'How did she sound?'

'Bad. And tired. Very, very tired.'

'Everything ok Mr. Abdullah?' Kumudini tried to gauge if the phone call was bad news or not.

'Yes, thank you Kumudini. Just some news from home.'

'Nothing bad, I hope.' Kumudini persisted in her gentle manner.

'Well, you know... no, nothing bad,' Abdullah replied reminding himself that the news was actually good. Khadeeja was safe and sound. Maybe a little traumatized but still, he consoled himself, she didn't know the boy really well. How well can you know a brother whom you have just discovered existed?

He wished that Khadeeja had called him and then remembered that maybe she didn't know his phone number. Maybe Raushen-Gul didn't have time to tell her. Maybe she didn't want to know. Abdullah put his personal fears aside and tried to concentrate on his work. But it was difficult. As he began to work on a memo regarding the rehabilitation work to be begun in the Amparai district, thoughts of Khadeeja kept flooding into his mind. Eventually, he pushed his pad aside and watched silently by Kumudini and Siva, smiled ruefully and said he needed to go home.

'Yes, go home Mr. Abdullah,' said Kumudini ever the nurturing spirit of the office. 'We can manage for today.'

'Thank you both and see you tomorrow.'

He left the room but not before he heard Siva tell Kumudini, 'Poor Mr. Abdullah. I think something has happened that has made him sad.'

46

Shirani Gunasekera stood on the verandah of Arjuna's house which once belonged to her father, looking out onto the neatly manicured lawn. She watched Christine speak to Swaris using a mixture of English, German and signs and wondered that he seemed to understand exactly what she was saying. She met Christine properly for the first time when she flew down for the funeral - the wedding didn't count. A nice young woman, she thought. I wish I had met her when Arjuna was alive. I wish I had visited them. I wish I had invited them over to meet me. *I wish…*

Regrets. Shirani's life seemed to be full of them. As her thoughts wandered she remembered that she had never liked this house. Now, she wondered what would happen to it. Would Christine keep it or sell it? Would she stay here or leave? She shook the questions out of her head as she saw Christine come towards her.

They were still awkward with each other. She knows everything, thought Shirani. She knows and she dislikes me.

'Lunch?' asked Christine and as Shirani nodded, the two women walked stiffly towards the dining room and sat clumsily opposite each other. Through most of the simple lunch they barely spoke except to occasionally hand over some dish or the other. After the meal, as Swaris cleared the table, he bent towards Christine and asked her through elaborate gestures if she wanted curd and *kitul pani* for dessert. Yes, she nodded and an absent look flitted across her face.

As she served the curd from its clay pot, first passing a bowl to Shirani, she began to speak.

'Arjuna loved curd and *kitul*. He told me that when he was a child he hated it and that it was only after he came to live here that he began to appreciate the dish.'

Shirani nodded. 'Yes,' she said hesitantly. 'As a child he couldn't bear the taste of curd.'

'Then,' continued Christine as if Shirani had not spoken, 'He began to make his own curd here on the estate. He bought two buffaloes, he called them Stalin and Lenin. They are still here, Swaris tells me. But he had stopped making the curd some months ago. It must have been around the time that girl - Khadeeja, came.'

Christine stopped speaking and raised her head to look at Shirani full in the face. Shirani saw her eyes brimming with tears which began to slowly slide down her face.

'Oh my dear,' she said, as she pushed her chair heavily away and walked towards Christine. 'There, there,' she murmured as she caressed the long golden hair and pulled Christine's head towards her stomach in a gesture of comfort.

Later as they sat on two *haansi putuwas* in the living room she asked Christine, 'What do you know?'

'Not everything. Just bits and pieces, I managed to put together from his letters, from Swaris. But it's very confusing. I don't know what is true, what is not. I don't know what to think about it all. I mean at this stage I don't even know if he loved me. He died after all when he was with another woman. Or so I have been told.' Christine looked helplessly at Shirani, her eyes swollen and red, her nose crimson with effort, her mouth trembling with exhaustion.

'Come,' Shirani told her firmly. 'You need some sleep. Come, let me put you to bed.' Obediently, Christine followed her up the stairs and lay down wordlessly on the bed. 'Thank you,' she murmured, 'He did love *you* though.' She said it softly, and Shirani did not hear it as she trudged heavily downstairs holding onto the elaborate carved banister as if she could draw some strength and emotional support from it.

Oh my putha, just when I think things cannot get worse, they do. Anyway I hope that you now have the peace that you were so desperately looking for all your life.

That evening while Christine slept, Shirani sat on the side verandah and gazed down over the familiar paddy fields. Her mind was blank and she was tired. Her face was drawn and heavy and her eyes mirrored a sadness that she did not know she could ever feel.

47

'What do I do now?' Christine looked at Shirani helplessly. 'What do I do with this house? You know the funny thing. I now have enough money saved where I can stay in Sri Lanka. I don't have to go back to Germany to earn more money. But now, for what? For whom?'

Shirani could not say anything.

'It's strange,' Christine continued, 'but that which is so certain in everybody's life is what is most forgotten. I am talking about death. We all have to die. We don't know when we will die and yet we act as if we will live forever.'

Shirani roused herself from her silence, 'Christine, we have to talk my dear,' she said gently. There is so much to tell. Arjuna was going through a difficult time in his life. Something in his past came up and he had to deal with it and while he was going through it, he died. I feel I must tell you what had been happening in his life. I mean, even I don't know it all, maybe Khadeeja knows more but I must tell you the little I know. It may make some things clear to you.'

'If you mean that Arjuna was adopted. I know all about it.' Christine sat up in the chair and brushed her dress down as she spoke. 'He told me once long ago and never mentioned it again. He never liked to speak about it. I will tell you that I was angry with you for a long, long time. I didn't know how you could do this to a little boy. He had no choice! Why didn't you stand up for him? If it was me I would have given up my life for him. What were you doing? You already had children, why did you want another child? You were greedy. You were selfish, only thinking of yourself. And what is worse, your family treated him so badly, where are his so called sisters? Do they care so little for a boy they thought was their brother? I can't talk to you properly.' Christine shook her head in despair, she stood up from her chair and walked towards the end of the room while Shirani stared helplessly after her in silence.

'I have too many questions and they are all difficult ones. As it is, if he was here Arjuna will be upset that I have said so much but I can't help it, I am sad, I am angry. I have lost him, not you. You never had him, you never wanted him. But for me, he was my world. I would have done anything for him and now...'

Shirani began to cry. Quick silent tears flowed strongly. I cannot say anything, she thought. This young woman is right. I took on something with trust and I couldn't keep it. She is right to be angry with me. For every action there is a reaction. For every deed there is a consequence. We must learn to live with them.

'Christine,' she sobbed, 'I have no explanation for what has happened...'

'That is not good enough,' yelled Christine with grief and anger. 'You will suffer. You are a Buddhist. You believe in another life. I will be very frightened if I were you. For what you have done is the ultimate sin. You have hurt another human being. Not just hurt, you and your husband have wounded the soul of another person. That is unforgivable. I did not like you but now I despise you. You are contemptible. I want you out of my house. Now!'

It was Swaris who prevailed on Christine to allow Shirani to stay the night. There are no buses at this time of night. She cannot leave, he mimed, there is no other place for her to stay. Let her stay the night and I will put her on a bus early the next morning.

That night Shirani did not sleep and for a little while she began to know what Arjuna must have felt like to live in a house where he was not wanted. *Oh my Putha, Forgive me! Forgive me! Forgive me!*

48

RaushenGul stood in front of the full length mirror in her room. She draped her silk sari neatly and pinned it awkwardly onto her shoulder. She turned around and tried to see how she looked from the back. I have put on weight, she thought. The doorbell rang and she knew that it was time.

I was sixteen years old when I married your father. He was thirty one. We had agreed that for the first few years of marriage we would not have any children. Instead, we travelled, went on holiday and enjoyed life in general. For the first four years it was easy to laugh at the old aunties, at my parents, at my in-laws who inquired at first gently and then more aggressively why there were no children.

'I know a good *pir*! He lives in the mountains of Hatton. Shall I take you?'

'Come with me to the ziayaram of Paani Kudi Bawa. I swear it works.'

Your father and I, we laughed it off. What do they know, we giggled to each other. We must first enjoy life, *then* we can have children.

After four years of marriage, I was ready to have children. Then when I did not fall pregnant I got really worried. *Allah is punishing me!* I thought, *but for what? For wanting to enjoy myself without the responsibility of children?* Your father tried to comfort me. It is Ok, he told me, but I would watch him when we went to parties, he was the one surrounded by children. There was a light in his eye as they clambered onto him and begged him to tell them jungle stories.

And then we started the rounds of doctors, hospitals, saints, vows. *There is nothing wrong with them, the doctors said, these things sometimes happen. There is no explanation for it.*

You will not believe it but if someone told me to do anything to get a child, I would do it. After six years of marriage I was getting desperate. I was depressed, taking it out on your father and every time I heard of anyone else getting pregnant, having a baby, the bottom would fall out of my world. I could not see families with children or a young pregnant woman without feeling envy and sadness. *Why not me, Allah*! I would scream silently. *What have I done that you have to punish me like this*?

One day, Nelum asked me to come with her to give her annual *dané* to the St Carmel orphanage. Or that's what she told me, I didn't know that Nelum also wanted to adopt a child but that they wouldn't let her because she wasn't married. So, anyway, I agreed, anything to get out of the house. Little did I know that my life would change after that visit. The orphanage is tucked down a little street in Matakkuliya. The wooden slats hide it from public view. As you climb the cement steps that lead up to a veranda you see that it is teeming with young mothers - unmarried girls who have got pregnant and who wait out their pregnancy, give birth and leave their babies to be adopted while they go back to their lives in the outside world. The air was filled with pregnancy and babies. The mothers to be, hung about talking in low tones, smiling, knitting, they seemed accepting of their situation. There was an air of placid contentment about them. It's funny that some who desperately don't want to get pregnant, do, and others who are desperate to have a child, don't. Do you think it's Allah trying to teach lessons? Do you think it's Allah's sense of humour? Anyway to get on with the story…

On the right side of the veranda you have two rooms that function as offices and on the left side is the first of many large rooms that have cots arranged in neat rows, filled with babies of all shapes and sizes.

I will confess that my heart jumped when I entered the first room …so many babies, wanting mothers…

I followed Nelum unthinkingly, waited while she spoke to the Matron, then walked behind her as we toured the orphanage. I think it was about three rooms down, closer to the end, when I saw a little baby girl sucking her thumb and holding a stuffed duck. Her eyes were topaz and I thought, *like mine*. And then I could think of nothing else. Nelum realized what I was up to after the first few questions directed at the Matron. She began to get worried, regretted bringing me at all. The Matron told me that the little girl was thirteen months old and that her brother had just been adopted that morning. They had been brought by a young woman three months ago who told them she couldn't carry on looking after both children. It was too much of a strain, she was not well enough and as if to prove her point, she collapsed on the steps of the orphanage. A few days later she died. The Matron said she would have preferred to have given both children to one home, but these days how can you be choosy. She was happy that the brother went to an affluent home, Sinhalese people, good people.

How many children do you have?

She must have seen the way I was looking at the girl.

Let me have her, I said while Nelum tugged at my sleeve and asked me if I was mad!

I didn't even ask your father, I just went home with her. It was easy in those days, no papers or bureaucracy, now I am horrified that it was so easy.

Today, when I think about it, everyone else was upset about what I had done except your father. He just accepted it; I think he realized that I needed this child for my sanity. She was my little miracle. This baby. She brought me peace, happiness, contentment and then the other babies started coming. It happens, they said, we have known this to happen in other cases also. Bring a baby into the house and the other babies start coming.

What I did, was it wrong?

49

RaushenGul watched her four children. She noticed that Khadeeja sat in between Sabrina and Tariq, as if she was in need of protection. She was normally the leader, RaushenGul thought, now she looks crushed, weak, we never thought it would be so bad. Why did we never tell her before? I cannot understand it. We were so foolish.

Saif, seated a little away on a stiff dining chair, rose and walked towards the window. He looked at the garden with such intensity anyone would have thought he was memorizing the flora and fauna that inhabited it; that had inhabited their childhood - the mango tree, the damson tree, the ambarella tree, the parrots, squirrels, konda kurullas, the koha, the shikra, the pol kitchas, the mynahs, the sunbirds, the hikmeeyas…

With his back towards his siblings, he asked the question that was on everyone's mind.

'What next?'

Khadeeja looked at her brother, the last time they all sat like this must have been when she was thirteen. Zay Saachi was preparing a *thala sholottu* for them. She was a crone of their grandmother - the Queen of Crones. There was Hai Saachi (in charge of the kitchen), Hib Achchi (in charge of prayers) and of course Zay Saachi (in charge of *thala sholuttus*). When they were growing up, the names of the crones were a source of great amusement to the children. What kind of names are these? They would question. Zay, Hai and Hib? Only to discover that their real names were Zaynab, Haseena and Hibshi. Not exactly servants of the households but more like powerful retainers they came and went from the household as they pleased, sometimes staying for weeks on end, other times no more than a few hours. They had all been brought up by Sara's mother and confessed an unswerving loyalty to the family that spanned generations.

Zay Saachi was summoned once a month to deliver the all powerful blow against any evil spirits that may have been lurking in the nooks, crannies or avenues of the grandchildren's lives. With secrecy and care she prepared her bundles of sorcery – red dried chillies, peppercorns, mustard seeds, rock salt, and an ice-cold lime would be carefully wrapped in old newspaper. After which she would wheeze, mutter, mumble and shuffle through a long and complicated prayer. The bundle rotated over all the children's heads in a wide elliptical circle, and then the ice-cold lime ran down each limb, eliciting a path of goose-bumps on their skin. Spit three times into the package and then special three eyed coconut shells were burnt with the bundles and the fire was read.

Tchaah! Michchum Kannoor! Zay Saachi's head would waggle from side to side in distress at the large amounts of Evil Eye that was indicated for these children of RaushenGul and Rasheed. After which she would crouch near the rear kitchen with Hai Saachi and gossip while delicious aromas arose from the open hearth kitchen that Hai Saachi ruled over. A fat square of betel squashed with areca-nut, coconut shavings and chunaam was wedged into a corner of her mouth and the two of them would chat, cackle and ponder the future of the world.

But now, Khadeeja thought sorrowfully, even Zay Saachi will

have no magic packet to whisk this damage away from us. It came from within us, it was created by us. It was we who brought it in from the outside, laid it on the threshold, stepped over it, claimed the outsider as one of us, nurtured and bred her, now who can take her away?

⌒

'What I want to know,' Saif whispered urgently to his brother and sister, 'is if she is going to inherit?'

'You know something Saif,' Sabrina whispered back, 'you are disgusting! I can't believe you are my brother.'

'Sabi is right, Saif,' Tariq murmmered conscious that RaushenGul and Khadeeja were in the next room. 'She is our sister, if Islamic law does not acknowledge that, then we must make sure that she gets her rightful share.'

'What rightful share? She doesn't get any, under Islamic law. That is not me making the rules, it is Islam.'

'Saif! you are totally fucked up!' Tariq fiercely whispered standing up. 'You of all people cannot talk about what is Islam or not. You bloody drunkard…'

'Shut up you two,' Sabrina always the mediator. 'Listen Saif, you do what you want. Tariq too can do what he wants…'

'I didn't say anything,' Tariq responded hurt.

'Shut up again. Just listen to what I have to say. I am quite willing to share whatever I get with Khadeeja. The two of you will make your own decisions and that is up to you. I know Khadeeja will be appalled that we are even having this conversation, if I know her and I think I do, she will not even expect anything from us. So Saif, don't worry you can hold onto your millions no-one is gonna take it from you. All I know is this was a reality check for all of us.'

'Ok forget about the inheritance part. What about the other part. The adoption part. I mean she is not really our sister…'

'Saif! if you don't get out of my sight right now, we will not have a brother. I will kill you if you talk about this now.'

'Jesus! Cool down woman you may not like to accept it now but I guarantee you that even ten years down the line, you will think about Khadeeja not being your sister. You will wonder about her real mother, who she was, a beggar, a servant woman, a freak? You two think that I am heartless and cold and greedy. That is not so, I am the realist here. It's all fine and ok to say that we are all one family and that she is our sister, but I know and you know she is not! She is not!'

50

The inter-monsoon had begun. The rain fell heavily as Abdullah's airport taxi thrashed its way to Katunayake one hour away. Driving fast but well, the driver had ceased trying to speak to Abdullah who preferred to turn his face towards the window. The rhythmic slap of the windshield wipers and the hum of the air conditioning cocooned him from the outside. He could see vendors huddled under flimsy tarpaulin roofs, pedestrians under a sea of umbrellas and sidewalks converted to muddy streams. Children with serious faces avoided stepping into puddles and only the dogs and cows ambled about without concern. Rain was messy in these parts of the world and yet, he thought, the rain that poured into the East Coast soon after the Tsunami was almost a cleansing in its own way. It was as if the heavens could not bear the destruction wreaked on earth and wept with grief themselves. The weather reflected his mood and suddenly Abdullah couldn't wait to leave the country. *This country. Khadeeja's country.*

⌒

Abdullah stood in the middle of the formal drawing room. He looked beyond the French windows that opened out into the verandah and saw the garden dropping below out of sight. An unusual house, was his first thought.

He saw a few family photographs arranged neatly on a low cabinet and he walked over to have a closer look. A happy family of mother, father and four children. *How we never know the real truth that hides behind families.*

He heard a sound, turned and his heart plummeted to the bottom of his stomach.

Khadeeja stood, small and delicate. Fragile, he thought, that is the word I would use for her now. She is so fragile.

He held out his arms and she walked into his embrace, rested her face against his chest and stayed there for a few minutes. She was dressed simply in a white shalwar kameez with pink rose petalled embroidery. Her hair was longer than it had ever been and was tied off her face. She had lost weight, her wrists were tiny and her fists were veined.

'Muli Bwanji,' *How are you* he asked her in Chichewa trying to lighten the air.

'Ndili Bweno,' *I am well* replied Khadeeja solemnly. They had taught each other their native language in the early days of courtship.

Holding his hand Khadeeja led him to the large ebony *kavichchiya*, sat him down and then sat beside him. She didn't utter a word. When she did begin to speak, her voice was cracked as if she hadn't used it in a long time or as if she had been crying. It could have been both. Abdullah wanted to take her into his arms once again, hold her close, comfort her, stroke her hair, kiss her eyelids and whisper that he loved her. He did none of those things. Instead they sat, holding hands and looking at each other, spoke in fits and starts and after two hours, Abdullah said he needed to leave to catch his flight. He wanted her to say *stay* and he would have, but she didn't and then he didn't know how to stay at all.

'*Tsalani Bwino*,' Stay well.

Ndimakukonda he wanted to tell her but didn't for he knew he would not be able to bear it if she didn't say that she loved him too.

Before this meeting Abdullah had been scared. He wondered if Khadeeja would want to see him at all. They had barely spoken on the phone and yet when he had called and said that he was now in Colombo and could he come to see her, there was a warmth in her voice that reassured him. He knew that nothing would be the same again for the two of them. Khadeeja had to deal with a lot and if she needed him he would be there, but it was something she had to go through on her own. It was a bit like starting over.

Before he left the house, as his taxi idled its engine in the driveway, he had a few words with RaushenGul. Knowing all that he did, he still thought that Khadeeja looked like her mother. *Must be the colour of their eyes*.

Then he left in his taxi for the airport. Khadeeja stood with her mother waving good-bye. Abdullah's heart stirred uncertainly with foreboding. He was not sure of anything. As the plane lifted up from the island showering shimmering green gold light into the cabin, and then dipped its wings towards the blue water of the Indian Ocean, he knew he was saying goodbye to love and he began to silently cry.

RaushenGul turned towards the house with her daughter. 'Come,' she said, 'I have something to give you.'

Khadeeja followed listlessly. The meeting with Abdullah made her feel even more miserable. She didn't know if their relationship would survive. In the scale of things, it had slipped to the bottom. Perhaps, she thought, it wasn't really love… who knows these things.

RaushenGul placed the bundle of wrapped cloth into Khadeeja's hands. As she began to open it Khadeeja knew from its shape and wrapping that it would be some jewellery. 'I don't want it,' she began to protest but RaushenGul urged her to open the package.

'Your grandmother gave it when you were fifteen years old to be given to you on your marriage. She didn't think she would live to see it,' RaushenGul whispered as they both stared at the diamond clustered bracelet.

'It's not right,' Khadeeja whispered, 'this should not come to me, give it to Sabrina or to any one of Yasmin Aunty's children. Ummi should not give it to me.'

As RaushenGul fastened it onto Khadeeja's thin wrist, she said, 'When I brought you home as a little baby, your grandmother didn't like you. She said you were ugly, that you were some half-caste child, probably illegitimate, with no lineage. She would visit everyday, say these nasty things to me, but always save a smile, tickle or a hug for you. Then she began quietly giving you her finger coated with sugar to taste, and feed you bits of chocolate and cake. All the time she would come and scold me for bringing you to the house and yet began to feed you sweets and sugar and soon you loved her more than you loved me. How you adored her. Maybe you do not remember this time, but when all around her was petrified as they heard her waist chain jingle ominously, you would giggle and crow with delight at the thought of seeing her. One day when you were about two years old, I came home and found you seated next to her dwarfed by her immense buttocks, clutching at her hips, learning to pray the Sura Fatiha. When I told my mother that I was pregnant for the first time, she was joyous but she also remembered you. *The child has brought the gift of pregnancy,* she said. *Don't you forget it!*

Khadeeja began to weep. Inelegant gasps of pain and sadness

ripped through her being as she felt yet another part of her heart cleave in two. *So much for me to know. So much for me to forgive. So much for me to love. And yet… I am not ready.*

End

Acknowledgements

Much of this book was written in Iowa, 2005 at the International Writing Program hosted by the University of Iowa, Iowa City. Thank you to Chris Merril, Hugh Ferrer and Natasa Durovicova in Iowa and to Phillip Frayne for facilitating my visit. Thanks to Gil Dryden for giving me Abdullah's story that captivated Khadeeja. Thank you to my readers, Chulani, Lisa, Mirak and Natasa for guiding me through choppy waters with invaluable advice, affection and encouragement.

When this book was almost completed I fell very ill. I was able to finish this book due to the immense love and friendship that many people showed me. For that I count myself particularly blessed. I am indebted to so many people there are too many to name individually but to each and every one of you I say thank you and God bless.

The following people who are thanked gave me support, care, friendship and the wonderful gift of love while I was ill. Thank you to Dilo, owner of the bright smile who often dragged me out of the depths of despair. Thank you to Sithi, Sunela, Chhaya, Nilmini, Ruwanthi, Lisa, Mirak, Ambika, Libby and Hafsa Uvais, for taking such good care of me. My healers Ranjan and Ali. My family – my wonderful parents, my aunt Budrey who has flown continents to be with me in my hours of need, aunty Anandi, Udeni, Salu, Zeyda, my niece Aneeka, who constantly inspires me, my grand-aunt Hafeela, uncle Farook and the two people to whom the book is dedicated, for all their support and love.

To Sam who said *do not thank me*, I do indeed thank you – for just about everything!

The following people who are [illegible] gave me support, care, friendship and the wonderful [illegible] with [illegible] all. Thank you to [illegible] owner of the [illegible] who often [illegible] me out of the depths of despair. Thank you to aunt [illegible] Shaye [illegible] Nawaratna [illegible] and [illegible] are [illegible] of [illegible] [illegible] and [illegible] [illegible] parents, my aunt [illegible] who [illegible] [illegible] of [illegible] [illegible] and [illegible] my [illegible] Aneka, who constantly inspires me [illegible] and the two people to whom this book is dedicated, for all their support and love.

[illegible] and [illegible] thank me, I do indeed thank you for just about everything!